"You've got a lot of people fooled about how tough you are, Carolina. I've seen you soft, I've seen you wanting," Brad said.

"That was one day. One kiss."

He smiled. "Want to try for two? Prove me wrong once and for all?"

"I don't have to prove anything. You've got flimsy evidence, counselor."

"Physical evidence," he insisted. "That kiss said a lot."

"Just a wrung out, emotionally fragile woman who flung herself into the arms of the nearest man. Forget it, Brad."

"No, I want to relive it." He tugged her into his arms. This kiss was blunt, explicit, full of expectations. She yielded, but only to sensation. She felt like a wild thing, obeying instinct, and that instinct was to surrender.

He tore his mouth from hers. "I know when something's ripe, Carolina. Talk to me. What are you afraid of?"

"That you'll kiss me again."

He grinned. "Anything else?"

"That you won't. . . ."

WHAT ARE *LOVESWEPT* ROMANCES?

They are stories of true romance and touching emotion. We believe those two very important ingredients are constants in our highly sensual and very believable stories in the *LOVESWEPT* line. Our goal is to give you, the reader, stories of consistently high quality that may sometimes make you laugh, sometimes make you cry, but are always fresh and creative and contain many delightful surprises within their pages.

Most romance fans read an enormous number of books. Those they truly love, they keep. Others may be traded with friends and soon forgotten. We hope that each *LOVESWEPT* romance will be a treasure—a "keeper." We will always try to publish

LOVE STORIES YOU'LL NEVER FORGET
BY AUTHORS YOU'LL ALWAYS REMEMBER

The Editors

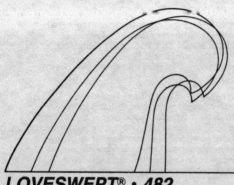

LOVESWEPT® · 482

Terry Lawrence

In The Still of the Night

 BANTAM BOOKS
NEW YORK · TORONTO · LONDON · SYDNEY · AUCKLAND

IN THE STILL OF THE NIGHT
A Bantam Book / July 1991

If you would be interested in receiving protective vinyl
covers for your Loveswept books, please write to this address
for information:

Loveswept
Bantam Books
P.O. Box 985
Hicksville, NY 11802

ISBN 0-553-44150-7

Published simultaneously in the United States and Canada

Bantam Books are published by Bantam Books, a division
of Bantam Doubleday Dell Publishing Group, Inc. Its trademark, consisting of the words "Bantam Books" and the
portrayal of a rooster, is Registered in U.S. Patent and
Trademark Office and in other countries. Marca Registrada.
Bantam Books, 666 Fifth Avenue, New York, New York
10103.

PRINTED IN THE UNITED STATES OF AMERICA

OPM   0 9 8 7 6 5 4 3 2 1

One

"Love!" the reverend thundered, and a hundred women's hearts skipped a beat.

"Love," he whispered, and the women trembled.

"Love." He reached his hand out to the audience, then drew it back slowly, fingers clenching, caressing the thick, heavy air of a Louisiana night.

Carolina Palmette walked up the center aisle, tall, sleek, in a silk suit three hundred dollars finer than anything a shopper would find in Grelickville, Louisiana. The light from bare bulbs strung across the inside of the revival tent glittered off the black alligator purse tucked under her arm. Brad Lavalier watched her entrance from where he sat in the front row, and something in him came alive.

Maybe she sensed heads turning, the slowed motion of paper fans, the buzz of crickets outside, and the dull flap of the awning overhead. If there was a breeze out there in the sticky night, it wouldn't find its way inside. Then again, maybe the Reverend Shepherd was all the hot air Grelickville needed, Brad thought with a wry grin.

He could imagine the woman in question thinking the same thing as she planted her heels firmly on the worn grass and dirt, never taking her eyes off the preacher. Earlier that afternoon she'd looked at Brad quite differently, the cool layer of confidence had been missing, outraged loyalty in its place.

"I want a good look at the no-account con artist who swindled Gram out of that land," Carolina declared, gripping the armrests of the imitation-leather chair in his office.

"There's no hard evidence of a swindle," Brad replied as reasonably as possible.

It wasn't unusual for problems to arise when settling an estate. During his corporate career in New Orleans, he'd seen many a civilized brawl break out over less. But Grelickville was different, smaller; he was closer to his clients here. He'd been sincerely sorry at Eve Palmette's passing. Despite their age difference, he'd considered her a friend.

He'd also heard a lot about the granddaughter—the proud, elusive, unyielding Carolina Palmette. She'd turned her back on this town once before, burned by a love affair, trapped by her own pride, ashamed to show her face there. The town gossips hadn't painted him a pretty picture.

But hers was such a pretty face, beautiful in fact—strong cheekbones, a wide, luscious mouth, dramatic creole coloring reflecting her French heritage. Was that why he'd waited three years to meet her? Why his heart pounded each time she pinned him with those hazel eyes and spoke in that cool contralto voice?

"You're saying Gram gave this reverend four hundred acres of land for nothing?"

"For him to hold revival meetings on."

"Gram was more interested in charity work than homemade New Age religions. Was he courting her? Filling her head with romance?"

"Not that I know of."

"But she talked with you."

"Often." But seldom about the Reverend Shepherd, he thought to himself. The elegant, elderly Eve Palmette had often invited Brad onto the pillared veranda of her home for an iced tea and hour upon hour of tale spinning. She'd intrigued him with stories of a granddaughter who'd moved to Boston six years before, a woman whose visits never failed to coincide with his absences, piquing his curiosity all the more.

In town he'd heard one story, from Eve another. She'd told stories about a passionate, vulnerable girl who'd refused to see how badly she needed to be loved.

Would the real Carolina please stand up? he silently asked.

To his dismay, she did just that, pacing his small storefront office, a gleam of late afternoon sun shining on her skin. She walked to the window air conditioner, stopped cold when hit by an arctic blast, and paced back again to stand in front of his desk.

"It's so unlike her," she insisted. "She was romantic, not gullible."

"She was a wonderful woman."

Carolina looked at him anew. "Thank you," she said softly.

Brad wondered if he'd ever get used to the squeezing sensation around his heart.

A frown clouded her features again. "Does everyone know she gave it away?"

"It's common knowledge the tent's been there these last three months. As principal heir, I thought you should be informed the land is not available for your use—as some details of the funeral have yet to be addressed."

"Bills, you mean."

"Yes."

"It'll be taken care of. I closed out Gram's accounts up North. She had me investing money for her."

"Sorry to bring that up."

She shook it off. "It's the land I'm concerned about. And the rumors." She smiled apologetically. "I know how shallow this may seem, but I don't like scandal."

"I understand."

"Do you? I suppose you would if you've lived in Grelickville long enough. We Palmettes are notorious for it."

He said nothing, but he thought—and felt—half a dozen tumbling sensations. Just as Eve had promised, the vulnerability was there, submerged in the soft, resigned way she'd said "notorious." But there was fire, too, and backbone, and all the Palmette dignity and bearing he'd associated with her grandmother.

She was a Palmette all right. And that meant she was more than just a client. According to Eve, she was his destiny.

Brad hadn't believed that guff for a minute.

He just wanted very much to put Carolina's mind at ease. To help. Men liked women who appealed to their strength. He was no exception. But Carolina hadn't asked. She seemed to think this was her battle alone.

"Can you break the will?" she asked bluntly.

Brad leaned back in his big leather chair and crafted his own question. Her answer could change a lot of things, knock down in one swipe the castle he'd been building in the air. Air gently spiced with her perfume. "Are you questioning Eve's competence?"

Carolina shook her head vigorously. "Gram was right as rain, and we both know it."

Brad concealed a sigh of relief. She was clearly more concerned about family honor than money. There was no reason that should please him so, except their whole future depended on it. Building castles in the air was one thing, moving in furniture was another.

"Seems the only other way to retrieve that land would be questioning the competence of the lawyer who drew up the transaction."

"And that would be?"

"You're looking at him." He winked, getting a startled laugh out of her.

"I don't think I'll be questioning your competence."

"Much obliged," he replied.

"And I can't make him pay rent for that land?"

"Shepherd? Not likely. He's got possession of it right now."

"And who has title?"

"I'm afraid that'll have to wait till the will reading tomorrow."

She didn't seem to mind his sticking to the rules. "So how do I prove a bogus preacher got Gram's land illegally?"

"Carolina," Brad answered, glad of the chance to use her name, disturbed all over again at the idea of her fighting her battles alone, "*we* will think of something."

"You're the only person in this town I can turn to, Brad. Can I trust you?" She reached across his desk, her hand on the sleeve of his jacket, her fingertips pressing lightly.

He nodded and swallowed, feeling the bob of his Adam's apple against a tight collar. The woman gazed at him, hazel eyes trusting—no, *needing* to trust. *Lavalier, if this woman were fishing for fools, you'd be in the boat flopping.* "You can trust me completely."

"And you'll keep this as quiet as possible?" she asked softly.

"Anything you want, Carolina."

She'd asked him for something comparatively simple; to meet her at Reverend Shepherd's revival that night. No wonder he'd been squirming in this tent like a restless schoolboy for the last half hour. He'd been waiting for his destiny.

He would've chuckled at the high-mindedness of it

all if his heart, pulse, and skin temperature hadn't gone on red alert the minute she'd walked up the aisle.

The organ music droned. The reverend intoned a hymn. Carolina came to a halt in the front row, eyeing the yellow wooden folding chairs. There wasn't an empty seat in the house.

Brad stood, winked, and offered her his.

Thanking him kindly, she sat.

And crossed her legs.

In the hush of the crowd, Brad could almost hear the whispered rasp of her silk stockings. He tried not to think of those legs or the way they'd moved in her tight skirt. At least lust was easier to explain than destiny.

He found himself another chair, snapped it open, and set it beside her on the aisle. For ten minutes he listened intently to the man who'd been wooing his clients away one by one. In the last three months, Brad had added a dozen clauses to wills, settling bequests on Reverend Shepherd. He was intrigued to see his doubts about the man's sincerity mirrored in Carolina Palmette's expression.

Her lips were pressed firmly together—coral lips, cool against her olive coloring and night-black hair. She was exquisite and exotic and aloof. She was loyal, fiercely protective, and all alone.

Having known her all of six hours, Brad felt as possessive as a junkyard dog. He was ready to fight battles, slay dragons, steal kisses. Shifting on the hard chair, he hoped the reverend's sermon would distract him from the steamier fantasies that had clouded his afternoon since she'd left. After all, a revival tent was no place for—

"Love," Shepherd murmured, brushing the microphone with his lips. "It can be the greatest force in the universe, or as small as a flower by the side of the road. Love of a mother for her child, or a man for a woman." He lowered his voice, paused, let them think about that one in the heat. "The only paradise we can hope to have is to find love on this earth. So why does it go bad?"

Heads nodded, paper fans picked up speed. They all wanted to know.

"I can't tell you. I can barely guess, brothers and sisters. Is it from indifference? A hardness of the heart?" Shepherd unknotted his tie with one hand, impatiently sliding it around his neck until it fell in a pile at his feet on the makeshift stage. The moving fans stopped, then started up again.

"The surest killer of love," he exclaimed, "is lack of faith."

Carolina glanced at Brad, aware he'd been watching her from the corner of his eye. She should have noticed him when she'd come in, the way his long legs stuck out in the front aisle, the way he'd unwound himself from a sitting position, white suit draped on a whipcord-lean body. She should have been better prepared.

Instead, her heart had jumped and her pulse had followed. She only hoped it didn't show.

"Why should it?" she thought. Her senses were overloaded, simply a result of tension and grief. She'd been jumpy and tired and, all too often, downright weepy since she'd got the news. Gram was gone. It was as if a Pandora's box of memories had opened inside her. Coming home had always been emotional. But Gram had always been there. This time she'd come home to an empty house, a family attorney she'd never met, and a charlatan who'd hornswoggled half the population of the town. It was no wonder her emotions were playing funny tricks on her.

"Do you have faith?" the reverend demanded of the audience with a shout. He pointed a plump hand at one man, then another, then straight at Carolina.

She kept her face impassive, although her fingers tightened on the alligator bag and her heart did a little flip. For a few infuriated moments that afternoon she'd considered denouncing him publicly. Fear of scandal undid her resolve. With or without Brad's advice, she'd bring Shepherd down legally, discretely, in a businesslike manner.

"Do you believe in what can't be proved by science?" Shepherd rumbled. "Love has never been proved. An EKG won't show it, no matter how full your heart or how empty. I ask only that you believe. Because love, my friends, is what I'm sellin'."

Carolina's mouth nearly dropped open. She stared at Brad in amazement, the first full look she'd given him since leaving his office. He smiled back.

"You find our friend here entertaining?" she asked.

He repeated her phrase inquisitively, in that seductive drawl of his. "Ah friend hyear? Never said he was mine. Said I knew the man." He looked her straight in the eye, like a man who had all night to do it. His legs were out in the aisle, his knees slightly spread. There was something provocative about him, daring and sensual. And Carolina was just short-tempered enough to speak up about it. "Didn't your momma ever tell you not to slouch like that?"

Brad's wide, easy smile answered her, in keeping, as Gram would say, with the man; open, easy, uninhibited. "I was six foot three by the time I was fourteen. It's become something of a habit."

"A bad one."

He let his knees spread a little farther, getting comfortable. "Cooler this way," he said, catching her quick glance at the juncture of his thighs.

She colored, turning hastily back toward the stage. He had the gall to chuckle—and to wear that white cotton shirt practically melted to his skin, revealing the ripples of his abdomen, she noted.

Carolina tried to get her frazzled concentration back on Shepherd. It wasn't hard pinpointing his popularity. He'd probably been devilishly handsome at forty and smoother at fifty. His abundant wavy hair was heavily grayed with the proper distinguished streaks. She wouldn't put it past him to help it along with some dye. Why had he come to Grelick-ville in the first place? she wondered.

"You'll be an old cynic if you're not careful," Gram had always said.

But Carolina *was* careful, that was just the point. She was the only Palmette woman to see that love, unless carefully approached, was the surest path to heartache and humiliation. Gram and her late mother had been quick to passion, loving completely and unhesitatingly. Carolina learned long ago not to be seduced by such romantic nonsense.

"Isn't that what gentlemen like this are supposed to do?" Brad asked quietly, leaning closer, his shoulder brushing her arm.

She wondered indeed what a gentleman like Brad Lavalier could do, but she'd lost the thread of his question. "What is that?"

"He's here to cure bad habits."

"If you believe he's capable of curing anything."

"There's no harm in having a little faith."

"Gram put all her faith in love. Look what it cost her. That land was meant to support the upkeep of the house she loved. Now it's been turned over to this—this con man."

Brad winced at the flash of pain in her eyes, reminding himself it was Carolina's home too. "She had her reasons."

"Which were?"

"I wasn't privy to all of them."

Privy. An old-fashioned word to go with the man, the town, the sense she had of sinking into a slower, infinitely smaller world where everyone knew your family, your past, your mistakes.

For six years she'd been gone. According to what she'd heard from Gram, this young lawyer had re-placed his uncle when Julius Lavalier had retired three years before. Exactly how much of her family's secrets and her own scandal-ridden past was he privy to?

As the last Palmette, she couldn't lose her family home. Not for want of money.

Coins jangled in a basket, dollar bills rustling like whispers. The sound brought her back to her senses. The reverend, having commenced the collection portion of the evening, stopped directly in front of her, the money-laden basket in his hand.

Brad got to his feet. "Reverend, I'd like to introduce you to Carolina Palmette, just back in town."

Carolina eyed them both. Charm, ease, and a smooth way with the ladies; they had that much in common, no more. Her trust for Brad Lavalier was as basic as her distrust of the silver-haired Shepherd.

"You wouldn't be Eve Palmette's granddaughter, now would you?" the reverend asked. "So glad you could join us." It was said with a trace of irony, seeing as she'd remained seated through the last hymn and the opening chords of this one.

For all his oily charm, this man had swindled a sharp if somewhat sentimental and romantic old woman whom Carolina had loved. Righting that wrong was her only goal.

"Reverend." Carolina nodded, her voice heavy with its own irony, for she doubted very much if that's what he was. The black clutch purse was open in her lap as she withdrew her wallet. "I'd like you to have this. A token of my esteem"

She handed him two cents.

Her nerves were still jangling from the confrontation at the revival show as Carolina entered the old house. It was as dank and dark as when she'd arrived that afternoon. She half expected Gram to call from the kitchen as the tall double doors closed, welcoming her home. Carolina touched her fingertips to her eyelids, took a shuddering breath, and let the emotions pass.

The chandelier threw shadows over the flecked wallpaper when she pushed the button for the lights. Despite the fact that she'd lived for years in Boston, she thought of this old house as home. The place was cluttered with as many emotions as antiques.

She'd air out the house, the next day, pulling the top half of the eight-foot-high windows down to let the heat escape, the lower half up to give cool breezes space to slide in.

She'd do it in the morning, before the funeral.

Brad had handled most of the details. She remembered his voice on the phone, gentle and low, tactful and kind, his slow drawl unable to mask the finality of the facts. He'd called to inform her Gram's heart had failed. Impossible, she'd thought. Everyone knew Gram's heart was the biggest, strongest part of her. But truth was truth, whether you believed it or not.

Carolina lugged her suitcase upstairs and found Gram's room. How could she miss her when the room still smelled of her perfume? Tortoiseshell brushes held gently curling white hairs in their bristles; a hand-painted bowl stood on the dresser, outlined by a spray of powder. If she opened the lid, Carolina knew what the powder puff would look like, how it would smell, how Gram used to dab her nose with it when she was being an inquisitive, too-serious little girl.

Feeling the sting of tears, she suddenly missed Brad's reassuring support. He'd offered to help in any way he could. That would have to wait until morning too.

Dropping her suitcase at the foot of the bed, she stripped off the hopelessly wrinkled silk suit and tossed it on the brocaded love seat. Gram always had been romantic enough for ten southern belles.

"This whole house is your trousseau," she'd taken to saying. "It's yours."

Carolina sighed. "Not without the land to maintain it, Gram. Not on my salary."

Money. Facts. Crisp, clear, manageable things she'd learned to control in her position as a financial consultant. They were so completely unlike the emotions, pervasive and flagrant and vivid, that were the true currency of Grelickville. The Palmettes had been an ongoing soap opera in this town as long as Carolina could remember. "Which is long enough," she murmured.

Peeling off her stockings was like shedding a second skin. Unfortunately, tepid was the coolest temperature the well provided for her shower. In the time it took to step out of the stall and listen to the water clatter its way back down the pipes, the heat wrapped itself around her like a wet towel and moisture once again dotted her skin.

She crossed the bedroom, opening the doors to the balcony. Holding a handful of lace curtain in front of her, she stepped outside. Her head fell back as she counted stars, the tip of her pony tail brushing the small of her back. Breathing the thin air of Boston, she'd forgotten how the heat could lie on you, physically touching you the way the northern air never did. Louisiana nights surrounded you, enclosing you like a lover's arm. Heat made you so aware of every inch of your body.

And that, for some reason she was too tired to trace, made her think of Brad Lavalier. Lean. Lanky. She pictured him luxuriating in this heat. She'd been away too long.

Shaking the clamminess out of the sheets before crawling naked between them, she closed her eyes and saw the expression on Brad's face when she'd handed Shepherd those coins. Even now she could feel her fingertips meeting the reverend's open palm, but the electric arc had emanated from Brad. She flattened the bed sheet with her hand, instantly reminded of the wrinkles in his cotton shirt.

Turning over restlessly, Carolina stared into the darkness. The twinkle of the stars matched the sparkle in his eyes; curious, piercing, challenging, and understanding all at once.

As more than one person in Grelickville said, it was the Palmette women's curse to fall instantly and hard when the right man came along. Maybe Gram had been tricked by the Reverend Shepherd, but he wasn't the man who had Carolina worried.

Unconsciously pulling back her shoulders and lifting her chin, Carolina was one Palmette who wasn't falling into anything deeper than sleep.

And dreams about the stars, winking.

Two

Set back from the small cemetery like a pillared mansion, the mausoleum was cooler than the day outside, the air heavy with magnolia blossoms and cut grass.

There was no coffin to sit beside. An urn sat on a marble shelf. Carolina felt closer to her grandmother at the house than here at this official place of mourning. "Sorry, Gram," she said aloud, startled at the sound of her own voice echoing off the walls.

"That's all right," Brad Lavalier replied.

She spun around.

"I suspect they don't mind a talking-to sometimes. It's a comfort to think so anyway." He ducked and entered through the low door.

"What are you doing here?"

"I thought you'd like to talk. Guess you were," he added in a low drawl, tacking on a sexy teasing smile. "Actually, your grandmother requested I say a few words at the service. I came in here looking for something to drink."

He spotted a spigot sticking out of the far wall. Doubling as a fountain, it dribbled water from an angel's tipped vase to a basin below. "I tend to dry up if I have to talk to more than four people at a time."

"I thought lawyers were trained to address whole courtrooms."

"Doesn't mean we take to it naturally." He smiled again.

With one foot on the marble rim of the catch basin, he dipped his head for a mouthful of nearly cold iron-tasting water, then wiped his mouth with the back of his hand. That did him some good. That Carolina watched did him even more good. He swung his jacket over his shoulder, holding it with the crook of a finger.

In the silence he tried to look her up and down without being too obvious about it. She wore a black suit—more linen to rumple in the heat. Her hair, straight and black, was pulled back from her face. The style was almost severe, he thought, until he noticed the French braid starting at the crown of her head, following the shape of her neck and finishing with a black bow between her shoulder blades.

He imagined braiding like that must take a good half hour. He pictured her hands in it, tucking, blending, her arms raised over her head, how the motion would lift her breasts . . .

As if tasting the same water he'd drunk, she licked her lips, self-consciously rubbing them together to smooth out the lipstick. Her mouth was as wide and sculpted as Sophia Loren's. He'd noticed that the day before. Somehow it had filtered in and out of his memory ever since, like a dream, hazy and erotic—like passion, something missing from his life too long. She'd been passionate in defense of her grandmother in his office and again at the revival. What else aroused passion in Carolina Palmette? he wondered.

With a whole room to wander in, he took the spot beside her on the marble bench. "If you don't feel like talking—"

"No. That would be all right."

Another minute of silence drifted by until she spoke again.

"I was thinking about when I was a little girl. Gram raised me, you know."

"She mentioned it."

"Did she?"

Brad thought her smile could light up even a mausoleum. "On a few occasions."

Carolina's hazel eyes grew warm as she gazed at the wall across from them, seeing brighter images of the past.

"Did she ever tell you about Grandpa Frank and his traveling days? Gram kept busy with charitable work when he was gone. One day he'd just show up after months on the road. She'd run to him. *Run*, mind you. The only time I ever saw her do that."

Brad's mouth quirked in a grin. Her voice was like cool water bubbling out of an angel's vase. He wouldn't have interrupted her for the world.

"For weeks it would be wonderful," she continued softly. "He was so funny, so freewheeling. But it always ended the same. Gram at the secretary in the parlor writing out a check, and Frank on his way again." Her gaze flickered, the memory dimming.

"Was she sad?"

"Oh no," Carolina corrected. "Not Gram. I'm sure she loved him until the day she died. It just wasn't my idea of what a marriage should be." She flushed a little. "Not that I mean to criticize; it was a long-standing difference we had."

"Not a painful one, I hope."

She shook her head, the black bow fluttering like a moth's wings. "Gram said, 'As long as love exists, everything will work out.' Come to think of it, that's the kind of thing Reverend Shepherd would say too." She sighed and shrugged.

Brad caught a whiff of scent, too delicate for perfume, hanging lazily on the humid air.

She turned to him. "Is that how he got Gram to deed him that land? A lot of talk about love?"

It took him a minute to answer. The words didn't matter, it was her imploring gaze that had his heart stumbling. He realized that if he waited for his pulse to come back to normal, they'd be there all night. What kind of man was he? Fired up about a woman who'd just lost her nearest and dearest, fighting flares of fantasy in a mausoleum?

The silent tongue-lashing didn't work. He knew the day he stopped responding to a woman like Carolina Palmette would be the day they planted him in Grelickville Memorial Gardens.

He cleared his throat. Twice. "I don't rightly know why she granted him that land, Carolina. Can't say I trust the man."

Neither did she, Carolina thought hazily, gazing into deep brown eyes that would've done the devil proud. Warm as a fire in a hearth and dark as the chimney behind it. What was that warning she'd given herself last night in bed? Something about not succumbing?

"If you want to talk about Eve some more—" he said.

And why hadn't she noticed the huskiness in his voice before? "Eve!" Carolina did a double take and swiveled toward him, bumping his knee with hers. "Since when do people refer to Gram as Eve?"

"That's what she asked me to call her."

"Well!" He was entirely too familiar, that was all. Especially when he grinned at her that way.

"Something wrong, Carolina?"

"I'll say!" She scooted down the bench, tugging at her skirt. "It was always 'Mizz Palmette' when I was around. 'Now you tell Mizz Palmette I want her to have this bushel of apples,' or 'Mizz Palmette's due at the social Thursday night, you remind her now, hear?'"

He chuckled out loud, tempering the sound for their surroundings. "You do the accent very well."

"Took me years to lose it."

"Ever want it back?"

What a question, Carolina thought, suddenly unsure of her answer. Looking in Brad Lavalier's eyes, wanting could apply to a lot of things—home, family, that anticipation Gram had bred in her that love was just around the corner, could come walking down the drive any day,

"And you'll be surprised, 'Lina. That's what love does, it surprises you."

"Carolina?"

"What? I'm sorry. Woolgathering." Cotton picking was more like it, as in out of her cotton-picking mind. She tugged her jacket around her and tucked back a hair that didn't need tucking.

"She cared very much about you, Carolina."

She thought there was something incredibly seductive about strength when it combined with tenderness. It shivered like the ripples of heat in the doorway, beckoned like the cool fountain. She'd expected to be alone and she wasn't. And she didn't mind at all. In fact, she felt calm, right, at home.

Of course, it didn't help that Gram seemed to be hovering over her, reminding her what a nice young man he was and that she really should try to be a trifle friendlier. Gram always said—

Gram! She'd be tickled pink Carolina even had spoken to Grelickville's most eligible bachelor. If only Gram knew what effect the man was having on her—the touch of his fingers on her arm, the caring in his eyes, welcoming, cajoling. And the answering longing she felt.

She missed Gram; it had to be grief. It couldn't be what it really felt like, attraction, interest, stirrings . . .

Carolina stood up so fast, her head whirled.

"Are you all right?" He was close, concerned.

"I think I need some air."

Before she could take three steps, he touched her, his fingers moving down her arm, squeezing softly. "This may not be the time or place," he said, his voice gruff but sincere, "but maybe we could have dinner sometime." His breath was minty and warm. "You can talk about it. I'll listen like nobody's ever listened, Carolina."

She felt the brush of his shirt when she breathed and knew she had to get away. She needed space, time, anything that would keep her from losing her head and crumpling completely in his arms. She needed him, but couldn't justify how or why.

"Comfort is rare in this world, Carolina. Don't pass it by."

It was as if Gram herself had spoken. Her words, Brad's voice, the evocative scent of mint, everything suddenly came together in a flood of memories.

He opened his arms. She gingerly stepped into them and let him hold her. He felt good, right. There was no reason at all why Carolina should deny herself one comfort.

A hug. That was all, she thought, letting someone else share the burden, someone who'd known Gram too. "I don't miss her all the time. Is that wrong?"

"No."

"It's as if she's still there. Here." And no doubt smiling, Carolina added silently.

There was nothing provocative about his touch, yet a tremor shook her. She'd never reacted to a man that way. Gram and Mom were soft. She was the strong one, the one smoothing over the whispers and talk, tactful and cool, sidestepping the messier emotions, ever mindful of appearances.

"Excuse me for interruptin', but are y'all about ready to begin?" The Reverend Shepherd stood in the doorway, a black silhouette against the daylight.

It took Carolina a moment to distinguish the suit and string tie, as thin and limp as his forced smile.

Slowly, she realized her position. Her arms had wrapped around Brad's back of their own accord, her body aligned with his. There was absolutely nothing to be ashamed of. She immediately withdrew her arms all the same.

Brad released her, not before his fingers skimmed the sleeve of her jacket in silent support—her right sleeve, which Shepherd couldn't see.

She appreciated his discretion. It didn't stop her wanting to touch her hair, her skirt, to straighten and primp. That would mean admitting how keenly Brad's touch lingered, and how badly, for a moment, she'd wanted to remain in his arms.

She nodded to the reverend instead, slipping past him out the door.

Hugging a man in a mausoleum! she thought indignantly. At Gram's funeral, no less.

Carolina sighed. Somewhere, in the hazy sky above them, Gram was probably cheering.

"I'm glad all of you could join us for the reading of the will. Mizz Palmette."

They were back to formal names, Carolina noticed as Brad nodded her way. She wondered if that was for the benefit of the reverend, who'd eyed them closely as he'd entered. Gram's gardener, Henry Soapkins, and her longtime cook, Dotty Willis, crowded the lobby. Brad ushered them all inside his private office, as private as a plate glass window on Bayou Street allowed.

Watching him amble around his desk, Carolina was sure his women clients found him charming and boyish. She was merely hot and bothered.

Ordinarily, she'd smile at the turn of phrase. Instead, she sat quickly and snapped open her briefcase.

Knees bent, Brad stopped halfway into his leather

chair and called through the open door to his secretary. "May-Lee? You can bring in the coffee now."

Carolina was running on little else. The funeral had been kept short, due to the older folks and the heat. The buffet was one long line of condolences and coffee. The reading of the will would mark the end of a very long day. At best it might send the reverend packing on the spot. She'd settle the household matters, appoint Henry Soapkins caretaker, and be back to Boston within a week, knowing the house would be in good hands for whenever she visited.

Then the reverend spoke up. "I get the feeling you're one of these people who doesn't approve of religion, Mizz Carolina."

Refusing to be put on the defensive, Carolina recognized the tactic from a hundred board meetings. "It's the messenger, not the message, I disapprove of, Reverend. The wolf in Shepherd's clothing, so to speak."

Brad tugged at the red square of handkerchief in his breast pocket. The tension inside was as high as the temperature outside. "Carolina," he said, rushing the introductions, "as I recall, you've met Reverend Shepherd."

"Yes, I have." She batted her eyelashes at him, southern charm in full force. "I was wondering if that was your real name."

"Arthur Winslow Shepherd."

"I meant the 'Reverend' part."

Brad coughed loudly and pressed a button on the ancient intercom system. "May-Lee? Send in the file now, please."

He drew a long finger over his upper lip to hide a smile. Carolina remembered the gesture from the previous night's confrontation with the reverend. She wondered if he reserved that glancing twinkle in his eye for her. He wanted her to know she had an ally. For some reason, that produced the strangest warming sensation in her blood, as if she were being held in two strong arms.

He withdrew a sheaf of papers from an expanding folder. "I believe starting at the beginning is best," he murmured perfunctorily.

When the reverend lit a cigar, Brad slid an ashtray his way without pausing. The air conditioner, undisguised by walnut-grained veneer, rattled and shuddered in accompaniment, wheezing out clammy, mildew-scented air.

Brad used the first paragraph break as an excuse to scan the room. He'd met Dotty and Henry at the Palmette house on different occasions. They treated Carolina like family. That fact spoke volumes about her.

So had Eve's promises. But there was more woman seated across from him than a photo and a grandmother's descriptions could hope to convey.

The woman sizzled when she walked. Did she know that? Or did she purposely hide it? Like the vulnerability, the softness was apparent only if a man was looking for it. Yet Carolina chose to play to her strength, from the shoulder pads in her suit to the briefcase on her lap. He hadn't forgotten the way her appearance at the revival had stolen all of Shepherd's thunder. She'd marched through that audience as if she'd been Lady Godiva in no need of a horse.

He'd wanted to march right beside her, and hold her when her steps faltered—as they almost had earlier in the mausoleum.

She needed him, but wouldn't let it show. He wanted her, but had to wait for her invitation.

Brad bit back a smile, listening to the drone of his own voice, aware of what was coming in the Last Will and Testament of Eve Palmette. Carolina, who expected to fight her battles alone, was about to be handed the toughest campaign of her life. The fuse was lit. The fireworks were up to her.

Carolina put two fingers to her lips. For some

reason the smell of Shepherd's cigar, mixed with the unwholesome air, made her slightly queasy. She blamed it on the jumble of emotions and memories, almost hearing Gram's voice in the bequests Brad read aloud.

"The house is yours." Brad indicated Carolina with a curt nod of his head.

She didn't write that down, keeping her gaze resolutely on the gold pen in her hand as her nails drummed a pad of paper.

"And all the land around it."

Carolina smiled this time and fought the urge to send a triumphant glance Shepherd's way. She might even buy him a box of those darn cigars.

"However—"

The drumming stopped.

"However, Carolina, that only includes the ten acres immediately surrounding the house."

"What?" She was conscious of trying—and nearly failing—to keep all emotion out of her voice.

Brad concealed a grimace. "There is an amendment to the will noting this." He flipped the long legal pages. "Three months before she died, there was a transaction involving the conditional donation of four hundred acres to Reverend Shepherd."

"For the tent show."

"I believe the reverend's organization plans to build a meetinghouse there. Is that correct?"

"It will be called Faith Church," the reverend intoned. "As soon, that is, as we accumulate the necessary funds."

"You mean he not only got the land rent-free, he now *owns* it?"

"Conditionally," Brad replied.

Carolina crossed her legs, balancing the pad on her knee while writing furiously. Her printing, Brad noticed, was neat, square, and even. The tremor in her hand was barely evident as she went on to the next number on her growing list.

She shot Brad an angry glance, as if he'd been caught cribbing answers on an exam. "Please continue, Mr. Lavalier."

"The house, as I've said, is yours with the provision—"

The toe of her shoe pointed downward as all five toes clenched at once, like a divining rod hitting water.

"Yes?" she said through gritted teeth.

"You must live in the house."

"Live there?"

"Some time will be allowed for getting your affairs in order up North. If you give up residence within a year, the house reverts to the reverend. And Reverend, if you desert the land within a year, it reverts to Mizz Palmette."

No one moved in the room. The day outside had grown dark with rain-laden clouds from the Gulf. The storm could break at any moment.

Carolina looked at her pad, then at Brad. "We'll talk later."

Brad worked his mouth into a tight frown and went on to the bequests for Dotty and Henry. The gardener balked at taking money he hadn't earned.

"Henry," Carolina said, feeling a trifle light-headed, "I'd appreciate it if you kept right on working at the house. There's no way I could keep up all that land—" She paused, peered at her list, and remembered with a pang that all that land was now ten acres surrounding the house. "You can invest what Gram wanted you to have, and I'll continue to pay you for your services. You, too, Dotty."

"Why sure, child."

"I'll see to it nothing changes," Carolina added for Shepherd's benefit.

"Is that all for us?" Henry received a nod from Brad. "We'll be going, then."

The reverend rose as they headed for the door, bowing chivalrously over Dotty's hand. "I'm sorry I'm being portrayed as the villain here. You will, of course, continue to do what you can to keep the house and grounds in the wonderful condition they were in every time I visited Mizz Palmette. He smiled, smoothing back his hair. "Who knows, I may be living in it myself one day."

The shark. Carolina bit her tongue.

Brad rose, the scent of his aftershave cutting subtly through the accumulated smoke. "That concludes the reading, Reverend. You have possession of the land already."

"Is that what's got this young lady's dander up so? Is this about greed, dear?"

Carolina got up slowly, speechless with fury.

Brad stepped adroitly between them. "Do you have any questions about the acreage, Reverend? The donation is conditional. If one of you leaves, the land reverts to Mizz Palmette."

"Or the house to me." The reverend exhaled a stream of cigar smoke her way. "Good day, young lady."

Carolina felt herself turning green and concentrated on how the smoke resembled the waves of gray in his hair. No chance that window opened, was there? She was the tiniest bit desperate for fresh air.

It would have to wait. First she had some business to conduct with Mr. Lavalier. In private.

Three

"Investigate him!" Carolina declared. "See if he's done this before, stealing old ladies' property."

"That's not quite stealing, Carolina. Your grandmother wanted him to have that extra land."

"Extra! Four hundred acres is not *extra*. She knew I couldn't afford the house and my condo too."

Maybe she did, Brad suspected, and getting Carolina to come home had been Eve's intent all along.

"People give him money. For what? There's fraud or misrepresentation there somewhere."

"If he sold your grandmother peace of mind and a place in the hereafter, how can we say she didn't receive it?"

Carolina wondered why the unspoken word "honey" seemed to trail off the end of his sentences. It had something to do with that drawl, deep and slow and sweet. Oh, where was her head today? "Will you do this for me, Brad? Please? I have to find out if he's done the same in other towns. That house meant everything to Gram."

"And to you?"

More than he knew, she thought. "It's all I have left of her. I won't let him get it."

Brad searched for something to say. He wanted to

explore the intriguing differences between the fantasy Eve had lured him with and the reality that stirred his blood. But that took time. The quicker he cleared up the land question, the quicker she'd leave. "I want to help, Carolina." Almost as much as he wanted her to stay, he realized.

"Then please look into it."

"I plan to." It'd keep him busy for a month at least. There'd be consultations with Mizz Palmette—after all, an attorney had to know his client's wishes . . . and dreams . . . and desires.

He patiently rolled the cigar Shepherd had given him between his fingers. It was a fine one, a shame to waste.

The flame of the lighter made the room flicker and spin. Carolina squirmed in her chair and concentrated on the next item on her list, running a fingernail inside the collar of her blouse.

"Want me to turn this up a bit?" Brad asked, motioning toward the humming air conditioner.

"No!" She got her voice under control. "It's a little clammy in here, don't you think?"

"Just another word for cold humidity. Can't seem to find a comfortable medium in the summertime." He gave her a slow smile and took another puff on the cigar, relishing the rare vice and thinking of others, equally rare, incomparably more inviting. "What else have you got on your list, Care-line?"

She was too tired to object to the pronunciation. All she wanted was to put things in order and get back to Boston. A matter of organization, that was all. It should be simple, would be when the room stopped tilting. "I'd like you to look into what we'll have to do to have the house designated an historical landmark."

"You plan on livin' there, Carolina?"

He asked it casually. She was just paying too much attention to the way his mouth moved when he said it.

"Not—" Not permanently, she almost replied, vowing to be more careful. The will said she must. "Under no circumstances will it revert to the reverend. Personally, I always thought it'd make a fine monument."

"Anything else?"

"Yes. Look into the zoning regulations, please. There's too much traffic coming and going after those revivals. That field will be worn to a mud patch the first time it rains hard. Would a permanent meeting-house even be allowed under the present statutes?"

"You do have a row of ducks for me to go a-hunting. Anything else?"

"Not for us," she said absently, peering at her list, oblivious to Brad's smile.

Next were the personal items. She'd have to get in touch with the office, explain her situation and get her files shipped down. There was a local brokerage in town where she could monitor the daily tape and stock exchange closings. Fortunately, the majority of her clients were as concerned with long-term security and low-risk funds as she was. They weren't the kind to buy and sell at the drop of a hat. However, she'd have to contact each one, explain things, see if they'd allow her to handle their portfolios via computer or if they'd prefer transfer to another broker in the firm.

Rubbing her forehead, she flipped the notepad closed with a quick sigh and returned the list to her briefcase. She had so much work to do. The Reverend Shepherd had the majority of the land—but he'd never get Palmette House. It was her trousseau, silly and old-fashioned as the notion was.

She sighed and sank back against the cool grainy leather of the chair. "Will you help me, Brad?"

He was sure she hadn't meant her voice to sound so breathless and inviting. Women in 1940s detective movies sauntered into private detectives' offices, settled themselves on desk corners, and spoke that way.

And stronger men than he found themselves wrapped around their perfectly manicured fingers.

Brad gave his tie a tug. "I want what's best for you, Carolina. Although it may be hard for you to believe, I'm sure Eve did too."

Carolina studied him. If she was enlisting his aid for something so vital, she needed to know more about him. "What exactly did you and Eve talk about?"

"You."

She swallowed, air and smoke going down together. "What about me?"

He shrugged, and Carolina had to concentrate on not staring at his shoulders, the hard planes of his chest.

"She told me about you as a child."

Carolina attempted a smile. "That couldn't have been very interesting."

"I thought I might have known you. I was here for a couple summers as a teenager, staying with Uncle Julius. It's possible we ran into each other."

Carolina racked her memory for a nephew of Julius Lavalier. Summer in a small town begged for diversions, and if a new kid was around— "Beanpole?"

Like the Cheshire cat's, Brad's grin appeared behind a puff of smoke. "Maybe I shouldn't've brought that up."

"You had glasses then."

"That corrected itself as I got older."

"Well, you're still— I mean you certainly haven't, uh, put on weight."

"Thank you kindly. You've grown up a bit, too, if you don't mind my noticing." He had done nothing but notice every time he was near her. And although he couldn't rightly insist he remembered her, he was damn sure he would have if she'd looked anything like she did now.

They smiled sociably, Brad straining his imagination to come up with a reason to vault over the desk and take a seat beside her. "A shame we had to meet under these circumstances. I did what I could for your grandmother. Unfortunately, the reverend came along. You know how she was about taking in strays. She thinks everyone should be settled."

"And a church building is more settled than a tent."

And a cottage out back of the big house was more settled than a room in a boardinghouse in town. Or so Eve had told Brad when she'd rented him Henry Soakins's old lodgings. He and Carolina were neighbors now. But how could he bring that up? He studied the cigar before taking another long drag.

"I guess I've taken enough of your time," Carolina said.

He stood as quickly as she had. "I'll stay in touch. About the case."

"And you'll check into those ordinances?"

"It'd be a pleasure."

It was all she could do to nod politely to him at the office door without pitching head first into the lobby. She was wrung out, plain and simple.

"Good-bye," she said.

"Good afternoon."

Back at his desk, Brad watched her walk down the street, jotting notes in his personal shorthand. It didn't take long to realize he was looking for a reason to go after her.

He was halfway down Bayou Street, the air as thick as corn syrup, when thunder clapped overhead and the rain came down. He broke into a trot, glad of the excuse, and almost collided with the Reverend Shepherd.

"Sorry there, son. Wanted to speak to you a minute."

Avoiding the rain, they crowded back into a storefront.

"You wrote up the papers for that donation, didn't you?"

"Yes, I did," Brad replied evenly.

"It was all legal, son, you saw to that."

"I believe matters brought to me are handled in an appropriate way. I represented the elder Mizz Palmette, and now I represent her granddaughter." In whatever legal matters Carolina might choose to pursue, he added silently.

"Then you're going to try to break the will."

"I drew it up. She'd have to hire another lawyer to do that."

Before Shepherd could breathe a sigh of relief, Brad pointed out, "Miss Palmette is a resourceful woman. More than that I'm not at liberty to say. Attorney-client privilege, you know." He winked and took a satisfying drag on his cigar before heading back out into the rain.

It cleared up as fast as it had come down, steam swirling off the pavement, sticky as cotton candy. By the time Brad reached the municipal parking lot, Carolina was crossing it with a small bag of groceries in one arm.

The wide smile on his face faded when she started to do the same. By the time he reached her, she was leaning against the car, head at door-handle height.

"Carolina?"

She stood up, blackness receding from the edges of her vision. "Got a little dizzy."

"The heat's getting to you."

"I was raised in this heat."

"Takes more than a couple days to readjust."

Waves of oven heat floated out of the car as he opened the door for her. "I should've left the windows open," she said.

"It'd be soaked if you had."

The vinyl seat squeaked as she sank into it. "It's got to be ninety degrees."

"Ninety-five according to the bank."

She didn't bother to look. Ideally, he'd leave, and

she could stretch out across the bucket seats and simply melt.

"Carolina?" He propped up her chin with a long finger.

She noticed how angular his hands were. Considering the rest of him, it made sense, about as much hazy, wavering sense as she was capable of right now.

"Scoot over," he ordered, lifting the groceries off the trunk. "I'll put these in back."

She complied only because she was too weak to argue. She didn't remember consenting to his driving, but as Bayou Street gave way to Three Mile Road, then Four, she knew they were heading home.

She switched off the car's air conditioning. "Maybe it'd be better to get used to it."

"That takes longer than the few weeks you plan on staying."

A little shock made its way through her frazzled system and she sat up straighter. "I don't recall saying that."

"You don't want to move back, do you?" He waited for her answer, counting on it more than he had any right to. Of course, a saner, more sensible man wouldn't have waited this long for his dream woman to come along in the first place.

"You sound pretty sure of your supposition, Mr. Lavalier."

Supposition. It tickled him the way people fell into legalese around lawyers, as if plain English were below them, or beyond them. "Think this town would suit you after Boston?"

The fast track wasn't the problem, Carolina knew. Grelickville would always be home. She'd run from it, as well as her own mistakes, but she'd never escaped it.

Inhaling, she dragged in some of the thick air passing by the window. Although the cigar was long gone, the aroma clung.

"You want me to check on how you can get out of the requirement?" he asked gently.

"That was on my list."

"I can tell you right now—"

But one glance told him she was in no shape to hear it. She pressed two red-painted nails lightly to her lips as they bounced down the rutted road to the Palmette house.

Pulling in the drive, Brad cruised past the tall front doors, taking her around the back to the shaded back porch. "Home."

She leaned her head against the headrest, eyelids heavy. She felt wilted, wasted, and wet, and she wanted to peel off her clothes. Her hair wasn't right. The shoulder pads in her suit weighed her down as if two hands were resting there. And the house . . .

It wasn't really home. It had been, it could be, but right now it was an empty old house, and she dreaded going in alone. "Could we just sit here a minute?"

"Sure."

The yard glistened with rain and muzzy heat. Spanish moss draped from the branches of a towering cypress like tattered dresses hung out to dry. Flowering vines and lush midsummer foliage were gradually swallowing the gardener's cottage on the edge of the back lawn. It was a cozy stone house—also empty, Carolina thought with a pang.

"I used to worry about Gram living out here all alone."

"She wasn't."

"Since Henry moved into town, I mean."

If Eve hadn't mentioned the new arrangement, who was he to?

"It can be a lonely place," Carolina murmured.

"Were you lonely as a child?"

"Dotty was here three days a week. Henry. And Gram."

"And Grandpa Frank."

"And Grandpa Frank." She smiled.

"But Frank loved Eve. Who loved you, Carolina?"

She knew he was getting at something, but she was too tired to ask. "This conversation keeps winding back to me. I wasn't trying to make you feel sorry for me. If you knew Gram, you'd know I wasn't a neglected child."

"But lonely sometimes."

"Sometimes."

"And now?"

"Not right this minute." She smiled indulgently, so relaxed, she could barely move. Yes, he was close, he couldn't help but be, it wasn't a large car. She honestly didn't mind his attempt to take her mind off the rest of the day.

"You involved with anyone up North?" he asked, trying to make the question sound casual.

She shook her head lazily. "Nope. Am I keeping you from your office?"

"That's your northern pace talking."

"Slow day, huh?"

"You were my last appointment. I'm in no hurry."

Eyes closed, she smiled again. "That must be nice."

She would look like that in bed, Brad thought, sleepy and sated. He tugged his tie to the third button and unbuttoned his collar. "Warm in here."

"Very. Thanks for rescuing me, by the way."

"Any time."

"I'm still a little light-headed. I should take a nap."

Brad fought down a groan at the picture that presented, and stretched one arm along the back of her seat. The headrest got in the way of a perfectly good high school move, so he dangled his elbow over the back, his hand just touching her shoulder. "Your suit looks hot."

"Mmm, it is. Maybe I should get out of these clothes."

His unmistakable moan opened her eyes.

Caught, he laughed. "I could've made that sugges-tion myself, but I was afraid of getting slapped."

She shook her head. "You're getting my mind off my troubles. That's sweet of you."

"I thought it was the gentlemanly thing to do."

"Distracting me or undressing me?"

If he could have crossed his legs in this Japanese matchbox, he would have. His fingers skimmed the back of her braid. "You might be more comfortable if we loosened some of this."

"Go on, counselor."

"I'm serious."

And she wasn't. A lady would have made that clear from the outset. A little harmless flirting was one thing, but he might misconstrue it. Carolina gath-ered what strength she had and lifted her head. "Brad."

"Shh. Rest a bit."

She examined him in the quite of the car. He had a natural tan, remnants of French blood. A faint beard, the same jet black as his hair, shadowed his jaw. She imagined it whispering if she ran her hand over his cheek, caressing him the way his gaze seemed to caress her, the way the heavy air had touched her skin the night before on the balcony.

The space behind her ear tickled. It wasn't a loose hair. There were no hairs there, except the tiny, sensitive ones slowly rising to attention as Brad skimmed her neck with his fingertips.

She stirred. He stopped. But not for long. He outlined the edge of her ear with one long finger. She wasn't quite so relaxed anymore. She was every bit as loathe to go in the house alone, but not tired.

"Maybe I should go in," she said, her voice breath-less.

"Maybe we can talk about that."

Going in? Or him coming with her? She was awake now, and tense. But the tension she knew usually started at the back of her neck and worked its way down between her shoulder blades. This tension started deeper, flowing, unraveling, skittering across her skin like leaves blown across a sidewalk in the fall, sizzling to the surface in surprising flares. A brisk Boston wind met a languid Louisiana afternoon.

As someone once said, South wasn't a direction, it was a state of mind. Hers was decidely murky.

"There's nothing to talk about," she said cautiously.

"You're thinking of going. I want you to stay."

"I have to stay. Because of the house. The will."

"I meant here. Stay for a minute."

His face was inches away. He had no intention of forcing her, but he was in no hurry to seduce her either. He'd let her own imagination do that.

A bird chirped.

The sound got her moving. "I should go in," she said more firmly.

He reached across her lap.

The door handle clunked, and he pushed it open. "Go ahead."

Even as he urged her out with a short nod, the sparkle in his eyes belied his good intentions. *Come on, risk it,* his eyes seemed to say.

Risk it. But it was only lust, engendered by the heat, the sensuality that went hand in hand with the need to shed clothing and stretch out somewhere, prone, willing, unencumbered by inhibitions. Persuasive eyes, permissive desires. All of it could be squelched by one high heel planted on wet grass.

She got out of the car. "Thank you again for the ride."

He didn't get out, not at first. He watched her walk, memorizing the movement of her slim skirt as she climbed the three wooden steps, crossed the porch, and opened the screen, fumbling in her purse for the key.

"You feeling all right now?" he asked from the bottom of the stairs.

Surprised, she turned. "I can manage, thank you."

"Aren't you forgetting something?"

Her common sense, maybe. Her barriers. He could almost see the gears grinding as she came up with another excuse to send him on his way. "Your groceries," he said.

As he headed back to the car, he heard her unlocking the kitchen door. She didn't open it. That might lead to inviting him in, and she wasn't about to offer. She'd wait until she had the groceries safely in hand, then she'd duck inside with some polite send-off.

So he took his time, ascending the stairs one maddeningly slow step at a time. She held out her arms. He swung the bag over to an antique milk churn and set it down.

She lowered her arms quickly, crossed them, uncrossed them, patted the sides of her skirt.

"You won't be inviting me in," he said, doing the hard work for her.

"I'm sorry, I'm a little worn out."

"A shower would be nice."

"Yes. It would."

She imagined being naked, the cool water refreshing her. She had the unsettling feeling he saw the same picture.

A raindrop spattered at her feet, and she started. "That must have got caught in the slates."

"An orphan of the storm," he murmured.

"I suppose it's bad for groceries, this heat."

"Suppose so." He continued to stand between her and the bag. "Think you'll be okay?" He'd never take advantage of a woman in real distress.

"Oh yes." She pulled back her shoulders and put on a smile. "I'm much better, really."

"No fainting?"

"I'm just fine."

Good, he thought, that meant he could kiss her.

Four

All along the timing hadn't been right. The reading of a will was no place to kiss a woman. Nor was a funeral, although he'd squeezed her hand, offered his assistance. Without intending it, he'd even gotten her in his arms. She'd trusted him enough to reveal a rare vulnerability. Only a conniving son of a gun would take advantage of that.

Or so the honorable part of him insisted at the time. The less honorable part chimed in with phrases like *Seize the day.* She'd made it plain she wasn't planning on staying in Grelickville if she could help it. And he was the man to help her get that wish. Provided along the way he got his. This dream he'd been dreaming, ever since Eve, was about to come true. He lowered his mouth to hers.

Heaven help her, but she was glad. Carolina's arms lifted to his sides before the first taste of him registered.

That Brad Lavalier could kiss, really kiss, came as no surprise. She'd had so many bad surprises—from Gram's death to the will. Was it a sin to want to hold on to a good one? To cling to it? Things made sense when he touched her, simple man-and-woman sense.

His tongue flitted between her teeth, and she

kissed him back. He tasted faintly of coffee and tobacco.

A murmur of satisfaction, uttered deep in his throat, rumbled inside her like receding thunder. Her mouth sought it out, tracing that shivery vibration over the ragged shadow on his jaw, her tongue darting out to taste.

She shivered like charged air. She'd be leaving when the details of the land were settled. This was a simple thank-you; she had no business wanting more.

He lifted his head. "Anything the matter, sugar?"

Sugar was the matter. All that sweetness melting like caramel in her bones. He kissed her, not as if he wanted to, but as if she needed him to. And she did. She did.

"Good Lord," she said, lowering her heels to the porch.

He crooked a brow. "Was it that good?"

"I, uh, my!" She tried to work up a smidgen of propriety, indignation. Like the rickety old cannon on the courthouse lawn, she just wasn't sure in which direction to aim—at him or herself. She didn't make a habit of kissing men's throats. And yet, even as she stepped back, her body felt deprived.

His hand whispered down the lapel of her jacket, his thumb hushed along the satin lining. Sensations rocketed through her when that thumb grazed the tip of her breast, glancing, asking.

She might have answered him if her derriere hadn't come up against the porch rail, which almost gave way. "Oh!"

He steadied her, the moment broken.

"That, that was kind of you," she said, wrapping it all up and handing it back to him.

"Kindness had nothing to do with it," he murmured wryly, wiping his jaw with an open palm. Without a mirror he couldn't say whether his eyes held the same frustration as hers.

Once more the timing wasn't right.

The woman was meant to be kissed. On hot days, cool days, most any night. The love they'd make didn't bear thinking about, not if he intended returning to the office.

His shoes sounded hollowly on the wooden steps, then crunched on the seashell gravel of the drive, snapping across the sultry silence.

If he'd wanted to put some color back in her cheeks, he'd succeeded. She stood at the wavering rail, surrounded by viney flowers of deep purple, their yellow centers laden with pollen.

For honey making, he thought, swallowing the taste of her.

"You'll look into that list now," she called softly, as he was halfway to the rental car.

He nodded. "I'll have May-Lee and her husband drop off the car after work."

"Thank you kindly."

He would have reminded her to get out of those clothes, but he didn't trust his voice, or his body. Or the last of his honorable intentions. One move, one sign from her, and he'd be back up on the porch.

As he started the car, the slap of the screen door brought his head around. She'd disappeared inside, into that big empty house that had more bedrooms than one woman could find uses for.

He thought the roar was his pulse until the red needle of the tachometer passed four thousand r.p.m. He eased off the gas and put it in gear, pulling out of the drive without a backward glance.

So what if she was headed toward a cool shower? She hadn't invited him in.

In your dreams, Lavalier.

He woke with the sheets scrabbled around him as if he'd wrestled alligators in his sleep. The clock read midnight. Apparently he'd gotten a lot of dreaming done in an hour. It was nothing compared to what he saw when he flipped over to switch on the lamp.

His hand froze, his breath caught. A light was on at Palmette House.

Cautiously, he stood, easing himself off the bed inch by inch, all the time aware there was no way on earth she'd hear a creak. His cottage was a hundred feet back from the house, a hundred feet from Carolina standing on her balcony, backlit by the bedroom light, naked as the day she was born.

"No baby was ever born looking like that," Brad muttered.

The light and the lace curtain left her silhouetted in shadow, until she stepped farther out, letting the crescent moon tip her skin a translucent milky white.

She turned to it, catching a breeze. Lifting her arms, she ran splayed fingers through ebony hair, revealing the nape of her neck to the sky. Then she lowered them, cupping her breasts in her hands, as if offering them to the moon. To him.

Sense told him she was waiting for another breeze, one to cool the perspiration collected where her breasts weighed heavy. She'd be salty and sweet there. Brad licked his lips and groaned.

Having broken the silence, he almost blamed himself for breaking the spell. She sidled leisurely back into her room and turned off the light. She was going to sleep—not something he'd be doing after that vision.

"Suppose y'all could go stand under her window and howl a bit," he murmured, slipping into a deep country accent he rarely used.

He wandered over to the bathroom door, contemplating the shower stall as the fluorescent light flicked and hummed.

"Mizz Carolina, you are a walking one-woman heat wave. And ain't that the truth."

• • •

At the end of two weeks, Carolina had called every client there was to call, arranged every transfer and commission split. The vice president wasn't too happy with her indefinite time frame for returning to Boston. Neither was she. His muttered "You're usually so reliable, Carolina," hung over her head for days.

Meetings with Brad Lavalier weren't proceeding satisfactorily either. There was the memory of that kiss, for one thing. She'd been very vulnerable that day, weak with the heat, drained from the funeral, stunned by the will reading. That he could have taken further advantage and hadn't was one point in his favor.

That she would have let him was a sizable demerit against her own judgment.

She blamed it on the easygoing sensuality that pervaded the very air, perfuming it with honeysuckle. The only cure for this constant physical awareness, short of a cold snap or hightailing it back up North, was hard work.

And yet, dusting Gram's antiques during her Saturday housecleaning, she found herself fighting memories of their last meeting. All her frustration had culminated in a snippy comment she'd made to him Thursday, something about his client list being made up almost entirely of senior citizens—the same as the reverend's.

"I enjoy the older folks," he'd said, hooking a thumb in a suspender while leaning against the lamppost outside his office. How he managed to do it without looking like an imitation Clarence Darrow, junior grade, Carolina didn't know.

"I'm fond of older people, as I was of your grandmother. But what about you? Do you enjoy your job, sugar? Like the people you work with?"

She'd blinked at the endearment, convinced it was

unintentional, relieved to be discussing something as basic as careers. "I have a few long-term clients, accounts I've had since I began financial consulting. I worry about them," she'd admitted with a faintly self-conscious smile. "A lot of them are older, and this is their retirement money. I look after it, kind of the way you looked after Gram. Thank you again."

"You're welcome, sugar."

That time he'd meant to say "Sugar." She saw it in his eyes—eyes that seemed to see right through every bit of clothing she could bear to put on this morning. She straightened her suit jacket. "Well. If we have no more to discuss."

"What about Eve? Do you miss her?"

Edging away didn't seem quite polite when he asked so sincerely.

"What I mean, Carolina," he drawled pleasantly, "is that it must get kind of lonely in that big old house."

"As a matter of fact, I miss her less there. It's as if she's all around. There are times, though . . ."

"You want to talk to her?"

"Mmm-hmm." He did have a kind streak, a soothing way about him.

"Talk about what?" he'd asked.

He leaned on an outstretched arm, palm flat against the office brickwork, his other hand balanced on a hip. His suit coat had draped open, making her very aware of the body inside it. And he knew it, judging from the twinkle in his eye.

All right, Carolina decided. If the man wanted to flirt, there wasn't much harm in it. "I'd like to ask her about you," she said directly. Maybe she could turn the tables.

"There isn't much she could tell you that I wouldn't gladly impart. Over dinner perhaps." When he got no response, he leaned forward and gently teased, "What would you ask your Gram about me?"

A lot of things, she thought, such as what to do when a man looked at her the way Brad did on a public street. Somewhere in her grown-up head she'd known the answer, but it didn't compute. Not when a thousand tiny fireflies were flitting up and down her skin.

She fanned herself with some paperwork he'd handed her on the way out of the office. "You know, Mr. Lavalier, you act as if you see right through me."

"Do I?"

"Mind if I ask what exactly Gram told you about *me*? The truth now."

"She said I'd love you if I met you."

His statement hung in the air.

"Tell me, sugar, did we ever set a date for dinner?"

They hadn't, and she didn't plan to either.

At home two days later, she banged the dustpan against the wastebasket until she thought she'd dent it. "Thanks for playing matchmaker, Gram," she muttered.

The people in town were no better, she thought— all those remarks at the brokerage about his single status, all those knowing looks when she came out of his office. "Got 'em all under his spell," she said aloud, swatting at dust balls as if they could bite.

She scowled, knowing exactly what people thought of her and all the Palmettes before her—foolish, overly fond, impulsive women defined by their love lives. She wasn't about to prove them right now. No matter how Gram had polished up the legend for Brad Lavalier.

Carolina kicked back a carpet to sweep under it. The heavy Oriental rugs should have been taken up when summer started; they absorbed heat like the velvet curtains.

She opened the fan window at the end of the upstairs hall and shook dust off the mop, watching it filter down in the evening light. It was later than she'd thought, and she was suddenly truly hungry for the first time in days.

She'd been a different kind of hungry two weeks ago in Brad's arms. "And dizzy. And nuts," she muttered, hustling the mop into the closet. No wonder he believed what Gram told him.

She collapsed on the parlor sofa, leaving the tall windows open, waiting for the heat to dissipate. Not yet adjusted to Louisiana's midsummer climate, she often found a languid, daydreamy fatigue overtaking her early in the evenings, leaving her feeling bedraggled and untethered, like a wilted balloon.

She tried not to think about the perspiration trickling down the valley between her breasts, tried to avoid thinking about Brad—his mouth, his hands, that loose-jointed walk of his, the solid body, his willingness to listen.

It seemed as if every time she so much as got him on the telephone, he had her reminiscing about something. As a result, cleaning house had failed dismally as a method to chase him from her mind. Touching the things Gram lived with and loved, she wanted to mention them to Brad. The story behind this one, the memories attached to that.

With an irritated sigh, Carolina flicked on an old standing lamp and settled down with a day-old *Wall Street Journal*. The distant sound of Shepherd's revival service wafted over the flat land, mingled with the sounds of bullfrogs and calling birds. Carolina could just make out the rise and fall of the man's voice.

"Should be a noise ordinance of some kind," she said suddenly. She'd call Brad.

The receiver was almost to her ear when she set it back down. It was late. And she was too eager to talk.

Taking a bath did little to refresh her. She slipped on a nightgown and lightweight robe and went back to the parlor. On the sofa, she let her eyes close only for a moment.

Brad stood before her, inclining his head to listen, to kiss. His shirt was loose and white. He wore suspenders, pleated slacks. All of his clothes were loose and cool, unlike the sinewy, heated body she knew was inside. She itched to touch him again.

His face came closer, his voice beguiling, his eyes cajoling, exuding an easy sensuality, receptive, persuasive. They were alone. No one would know . . .

Carolina awoke with a crick in her neck, the newspaper on the floor at her feet. It was pitch-black outside, and she hadn't closed the curtains. The revival was over, silence reigned. And yet every nerve in her body was on alert.

Then it came again, the sound she'd been straining to hear. A swoop, a high-pitched squeak. A bat!

As it flapped wildly near the fourteen-foot ceiling, Carolina ran for the closet. "Out!" Swinging the straw broom overhead, she raced to the living room like a crazed piñata player. "Get out!"

She uttered an unladylike curse as her shin connected with the coffee table, and fought down a shudder as the skittering animal gave out one of its eerie little cries. Almost knocking over the lamp, she tried to remember if bats were attracted or repelled by light. She flicked it on.

Even if the creature didn't have the three-foot wing span she'd imagined, seeing it was worse. "Ugly little rat-faced thing." She took another swipe. Strike two.

It swooped low, and Carolina screamed, feeling idiotic and giddy all at once. Thank God no one was there to see her! The bat dove in her direction. This time her scream claimed all her lung power.

Despite her scorn for old wives' tales, she checked to make sure her hair was tied back so the animal couldn't get tangled in it. She tightened the sash on her robe, gathering the folds of the skirt in her hand. "Just in case it dive-bombs your feet?" she asked no one in particular. She knew she was making a fool of herself, but Lord, these things were awful.

"Aim it toward the windows," she commanded the broom.

The bat careened past her head and into the hallway.

"No! No!"

The last thing she wanted was to chase it in and out of bedrooms. The front door! she realized. Opening it would give the creature an escape route.

Before she could act, the door burst open. She let out a bloodcurdling scream.

"I thought you were being murdered," Brad declared, charging in, fending off the straw broom.

"Oh no!" she cried.

The bat flitted in and out of the chandelier, tinkling the crystals. Carolina chased it up the stairs, heading it off as it fluttered over the ornate staircase. "What are you doing here?" she shouted at Brad.

"Passing by." He followed her progress up the winding stairs, ducking each sweep of the broom.

"Go away," she cried to both her unwanted guests. "I can manage."

"You can wake half the neighborhood."

"There is no neighborhood. Except for that darn congregation tent and Holy Roller parking lot— Eeek!"

The bat swooped again, and Carolina hit the chandelier. In the crazily swaying light, Brad seized the broom as it whistled over his head. "You're going to kill somebody with that. Will you give me that thing?"

"I can handle this!"

"You can scare the poor thing to death."

"Poor thing? These monsters carry rabies, you know."

"So why make it mad? Does the window open?"

He jerked his head toward the fanlight at the far end of the hall just as the bat found the front door and made its escape. Carolina raced after it, slamming the door shut.

"That was easy." Brad smiled, ceremoniously marching down the stairs, broom shouldered like a rifle. Coming to a stop in front of her, he clicked his heels and bowed, handing the broom back with both hands, a sword of surrender. "At your service, ma'am."

Carolina, out of breath from screaming, shouting, and running up and down stairs, snatched it from him. She was in no mood to be teased—or charmed. But she couldn't help bursting out laughing. She covered her mouth to smother another whoop. "What a sight the two of us must have made!"

The comment, and his appreciative look, instantly reminded her she was half-dressed and her hair was in disarray.

Brad didn't seem to mind. His smile faded when hers did. "Good evening."

"Think you can sound any more like Bela Lugosi?"

"I don't know. I wouldn't mind biting your neck."

She recalled she'd almost done the same to him two weeks ago. That didn't stop her from pretending the blood rushing to her cheeks was only from exertion. And heat. "I suppose I owe you a cup of tea." It was the merest of social acknowledgments, but it afforded her an excuse to flee the parlor. Her heart was pounding crazily, the result of too much excitement—and the bat, of course.

"Much obliged," Brad called after her. "My heart's still in overdrive."

Carolina peeked out of the kitchen in time to glimpse him laying a hand over his heart. She imagined her own hand there, how the pulsing beat would feel through his shirt. How it had felt once before. Maybe she should apologize for that kiss, put it behind them once and for all.

She filled a teakettle and bustled back to close the parlor windows, giving the velvet curtains a shake first. "These should have come down for the summer. I'll go up to the attic tomorrow and find the summer set."

"Staying a while?"

Why did his question sound like some kind of sleepy-eyed invitation? "You know I have to. Not that I wanted to at first." She could be honest with him about everything but the unwanted emotions he stirred in her. "I was hoping you'd have me on my way back to Boston soon."

"So I figured."

"But things have settled down somewhat. My boss is letting me do a lot via computer, although the long-distance rates come out of my commissions."

Even with her back to him, she was aware of him shedding his jacket, tossing it over the back of a tall chair. Hands in his pockets, he watched her work the high upper windows. She reached up, hooking each with a long wooden cue, a metal attachment at the end for closing the latches.

"Need help?"

"You wouldn't know how."

"I think I could manage."

He grinned at some double entendre of his own, and she turned back to the chore, wondering why her cheeks felt so flushed. Just because she was dressed for bed and he was rolling up his shirtsleeves and unknotting his tie . . .

Could it be that moments ago she'd been fearlessly fending off creatures of the night? Suddenly she felt as fragile as the chandelier.

The metal tip scraped the fixture again. Stretching and straining, she got the window closed, but because of her shaking hands, she couldn't latch it. "Early nineteenth century, this stuff."

Increasingly frustrated, it was either give up or set down the cue and face him. She fought the latch instead.

Brad watched her move. Seeing Carolina Palmette

out of a business suit was entertaining all by itself. Her hair was black as the night outside; the ribbon in her pony tail slack, trailing so far down her back, the tail end skimmed her derriere. She bent her head back to look up, as she had when he'd kissed her—as she had while kissing *him*, he amended, leaning against the sofa.

The lamp threw a mirror image of her on the long window pane. Her gown wafted around her legs. What his imagination instantly set to work on, was why she wore anything to bed at all. It was too hot, and he'd seen her some nights on the balcony wearing considerably less.

He cleared his throat. Coming up beside her, he steadied the cue with one big hand. By her side, he heard the glimmer of satin whisper against his pant leg.

"You don't ask for anything from anybody, do you, 'Lina?"

"I've asked you not to call me that."

He'd discovered her old nickname somewhere and enjoyed using it, but only in those rare moments when they were alone.

Carolina knew it was a brand of intimacy. Just as she knew it was a mistake looking at him when they were so close.

She suddenly realized her interrupted dream had been of him, the feel of him, long, tall, masculine, and hard; the gentle lure of honey and sweet words. It was a dream to hold on to, along with the admonition that all dreams ended in the light of day.

Brad latched the last hook with a quick flick, catching her startled look. "Many's a time I'd do this for Eve when her arthritis was acting up."

She should have guessed, but it was an easier subject to discuss than the two of them. "I've been wanting to ask you about her. If we can stay on that subject," she added.

He'd been wanting too. Brad put his hands in his

pockets, rubbing his fingers over some spare change, two pennies he'd been carrying for good luck. He tried his best to look relaxed, unthreatened, unaware of the tension in the room and how it all seemed to be radiating from him.

Like a gentleman, he waited until she retreated to the safety of the sofa. Like a cad, he said, "Easier than talking about that kiss."

She objected.

He overrode it with an upraised palm. "I like to think we both knew what we were doing. I hope I'm not the only one who got pleasure out of it."

Pleasure. Carolina swallowed on the word. Was that all people around there cared about? Not futures, not plans, or security, just pleasure and the heat of the moment?

"I wasn't going to mention it at all," she replied. "I wanted to talk to you about Gram and what she might have said."

"You heard what she asked me to say at the funeral. About a life well lived if a woman was well loved. She wanted you to find that."

"I appreciated your speaking."

"And her advice? Will you take it?"

He was persistent. He'd be good in court, Carolina thought. He'd be good in a lot of places. "I'm afraid we can't pick and choose who we love that easily."

"She said you were afraid."

"Of what?"

He shrugged. "People's opinions."

Carolina smiled as if setting foot on firmer ground. "I might have been years ago, when I left town. I've realized since there's not much I can do about what people think."

Brad figured she was going to convince him of that if she had to go upstairs and put on one of her suits. Self-reliant, competent, steadfastly single Carolina. She made sure everyone saw how confident and unbreakable she was. But she wasn't unbendable. She'd made that mistake in his arms.

He'd seen her in town since, always perfectly dressed. Her slim skirts hiding but outlining her long legs, the matching stockings, matching shoes. Any makeup she wore was so artfully applied as to call no attention to itself. Was that the look of someone who didn't care what others thought? "I got the impression you cared about scandal."

"Of course I do. I don't want Gram being talked about when she isn't here to defend herself."

"I don't recall her ever feeling the need to defend anything."

"No." Carolina sighed. "She was oblivious to most of it."

"Then it couldn't have done much harm."

"Not to her."

"And you?" Brad suddenly realized he'd been picturing Carolina as always having been strong, at least on the surface. Defenses like hers were learned. How many times did a flame have to burn you before you told yourself you didn't need fire? "What kind of talk was it?"

No one down South would ever think to ask such a question, and no one up North would possibly understand. He was listening again, giving her openings. Part of her ached to tell him. "I don't know when it started. I think it went all the way back to the Confederacy, women waiting for men who didn't return. In Gram's case that was Grandpa Frank. No matter how often or how long he was gone, she waited and she loved him."

"And your mother?"

"She tried to change the story. Rather than wait, she followed my father all over the South."

"Is that bad?"

"When there's a child involved, it may be. They parked me with Gram and kept going—all the way to

Texas and an automobile accident that killed them both when I was seven."

A moment passed. Carolina felt the old give, the sense that Brad was there for her, accepting, not judging.

"So Eve adopted you and gave you the Palmette name."

She didn't hesitate to look him in the eye. "There was no need to give me the name. I already had it. They were too much in love to wait for a ceremony. But those are Palmettes for you—blinded by love."

"And you?"

The thin robe stretched taut across her breasts as she folded her arms. "I believe I've escaped that fate successfully so far."

He questioned her definition of success. But there was another angle to pin down first. Something she'd said before. "Are children so cruel?"

"What? Oh." Why did he have to be so perceptive? "Teasing me about my mother and father, you mean. I was always torn about that." Her gaze skimmed the Oriental rug, complex patterns resolving themselves into a handful of large round flowers. Beauty and simplicity amid so many wanderings. Then she looked up at him.

"On the one hand, people acted as if I should feel ashamed. But Gram said happiness was nothing to be ashamed of, neither was bringing life into this world."

"A family that created you is nothing to be ashamed of."

Startled, she smiled. "You have a way of turning things into compliments. Making lemons into lemonade, counselor? Anyway, Gram always said I should be proud I came from a family of women who had the courage to love."

Her comment hung on the sultry air between them. "Do they?" he asked softly.

She sat on the sofa, pouring tea. He sat beside her.

Done with her hostess chores, she tucked her feet under her.

Brad didn't care how primly she normally dressed. Reclining against throw pillows, hugging one to her chest, she looked as if she'd spent the evening in bed with a lover. Her lipstick was kissed away, roughly or gently, he couldn't tell. The image had the corners of his mouth drawing down. How many lovers had she had? He stood and paced; somehow he thought better that way. "So that's the Palmette Curse?"

"That's it. A few star-crossed romances, and the next thing you know it's a fine old family curse. We Palmette women are expected to carry on the tradition." She paused, a quick frown of enlightenment creasing her brow. "So you've heard about the curse."

"People still talk."

"Yes, they do. What's true for one or two members of a family becomes destiny for the whole clan." She sounded resigned, but not for long. "Is that why you think you can kiss me and I'll melt?"

He refrained from pointing out she had. "Eve said you were afraid of it."

She fluffed a pillow that had become too obvious a shield and stuffed it behind her. "Do you know what a relief it is living in a city where people only know what you tell them? Down here people seem convinced I'll be just like all the other women before me."

"You don't want to be loved the same way?"

"I don't want it talked of all over town."

"Ah."

"It isn't easy going on a date and the next day having the lady at the grocery store ask you when the wedding is."

He laughed. "That's fairly harmless."

"Not to a sixteen-year-old boy, it isn't. That story chased off more dates than I can count."

They laughed together.

"Some men are more easily dissuaded," Brad

drawled, letting her know with no more than a slow glance that he wasn't one of them.

Carolina fiddled with her robe, drawing the silk edging together where it gapped. "Then there are the ones who believe in instant attraction."

"Meaning?"

"They think I'll fall at their feet if they so much as whistle my way."

"You won't."

"No, I won't."

"Then kiss me again."

It was a barefaced challenge. And Carolina, having stated her reasons so forcefully, felt perfectly capable of meeting it head-on.

She stood up. A pillow tumbled to the floor with a thud and a feathery sigh. Carolina watched Brad's throat as he swallowed hard.

Her robe skimmed her calves as she stalked patiently around the coffee table toward him. When she stopped, inches from his chest, her robe whispered forward, swaying against her legs—and his. "You saying I'm afraid to kiss you?"

He cleared his throat. "Guess not."

She touched a finger to his lower lip. His teeth ground tight. She could probably tell that by the vein in his jaw. Subtly, she drew her shoulders back, loosely linking her fingers in front of her. She'd made her point. "I don't care to fulfill everyone's expectations. Including yours."

She'd slipped out of his net again. Brad cleared his throat, taunted just enough to push his luck. "Seems to me you're still living according to what others think. Or else you wouldn't try so hard to prove 'em wrong."

"We slip into old habits when we return to old haunts," she said lightly.

"You care," he replied. "What you've learned is how to hide it."

"You're a better lawyer than you let on."

She wouldn't show the passion either, Brad decided. But that didn't mean it wasn't there. He'd seen it, at night when she thought she was alone.

He freely conceded his romantic streak, a willingness to drift, to dream. He'd waited all this time for some figment of Eve's imagination to come along and make his life sing. If Carolina wasn't that woman, she had only to prove him wrong. He'd be man enough to bow out.

And she was trying. He had to give her credit. Up to now she'd distanced herself from her love-struck past. It just wasn't working with him. He'd kissed her. He knew better.

He also knew that sooner or later he'd kiss her again. Sooner or later he'd take her in his arms and explore the softness beneath the surface.

Sooner was sounding better to him all the time.

Five

"How would you feel if I did it to you?" Carolina dared him.

He had to shake his head to clear the smoky cobwebs of desire. "There are a lot of things I'd like you to do to me."

"I meant, what if I believed the gossip about you? From what I hear, we both ran away from what was expected of us, you quitting a corporate job to hide out in this little town."

As she paced to the corner of the room like a prosecuting attorney presenting a star witness, Brad decided it was safe to take his hands out of his pockets. For a few minutes, he'd been dangerously close to taking *her*.

"I'm flattered you asked around," he replied.

"I didn't. People are happy to volunteer when there's a single man on the loose and I'm in town."

"Is that why you've avoided meeting me on previous visits?"

"You were just the family lawyer before . . ."

He grinned, watching the way she looked elsewhere rather than meet his gaze. "And what am I now?"

"A pest."

"A pest with a past?"

He was being playful and prodding. He could hide behind that harmless facade all he wanted, Carolina wasn't stepping into his arms again. For about thirty seconds she'd defied the sparks that crackled when she was close to him. Singed, she stayed well back and ran her tingling fingertips against her robe.

Brad filled in the blanks. "I burned out big-time on corporate law, and Uncle Julius took me in. Is that what you wanted to hear?"

"I didn't mean to pry."

"No harm. Your methods are downright gentle. You don't know the ways information can be extracted from newcomers in Grelickville."

"Gestapo tactics, huh?"

"Subtle as sledgehammers, but you're always served tea afterward."

She chuckled. "From what I've heard of your client list, you have some of the nosiest old ladies in town."

"All of whom are wondering when you'll pay them a visit. To talk about your grandmother."

"We talked at the buffet after the funeral. If I see them again, it'll be so they can unearth my marriage plans. Oh, I know them."

"And me?" He sauntered nearer. It was time to be as open with her as he'd asked her to be with him. "I wanted a life I didn't even know how to find. Eve took me in after Julius died, spinning tales delicate as spiderwebs, making me see what a man really needs in life."

He was looking at it—hazel eyes, flushed cheeks, the strength of a woman and the vulnerability of a lover.

"You believed her?"

He nodded. "A man know's right when he hears it."

"If he's listening."

"I'm a good listener, 'Lina. Remember?"

She tasted him all over again. Who was caught in the web now? she wondered. Her lips, pressed tight, remembered the insistent pressure of his; her memory sent off flares of physical sensation. She looked away, wary of calling up so many memories, so many dreams, worried he'd see them in her eyes, sense them in her quickening breath.

"But don't you see?" she asked. "Doesn't it make you uncomfortable that I learned all this without any input from you?"

"We can remedy that. Sit down, and I'll tell you the whole story."

She eyed the sofa. He made it sound simple, sitting beside him, alone, at night, his voice in her ear, perhaps an arm draped over her shoulders. And she could sink in that gentle voice, the easy drawl seeping under her fears, into her heart. Her resolve was as sturdy as a feather-stuffed pillow, her head as light. "People talk too much."

"Showing an interest means they care."

He'd shown an interest. Did that mean—? Carolina shook her head. "Small towns are just big families."

"It's a close-knit community," he agreed.

"And I'm the loose string."

"They'd all be more comfortable if you tied the knot."

She smiled grudgingly. "'They' meaning just about everyone I've met since I've been back. They all love you, you know."

"They'd love you, too, if you gave them a chance."

"Little old ladies love you."

"Mostly."

"Drunks at the jail love you."

"When I bail 'em out."

"Does anyone not love you, Mr. Lavalier?"

"DeVoe's dog. Chases me up the Quantico Road every time I go running."

"So it's either me and Grelickville, or I side with the dog."

"I'm a wonderful human being when you get to know me, sugar."

It wasn't the first time she'd resisted his charm.

However, it was the first time she asked herself why. "How do I know what you've heard about me? I get no chance to defend myself."

"From compliments?"

"From misconceptions."

He skimmed his fingertips over her cheek. "Carolina."

"The picture you have of me could be very incorrect."

And it could be standing right before him, quivering. "Don't bother hauling on the armor or pulling up the drawbridge now. You've got a lot of people fooled about how tough you are. I've seen you soft, remember? I've seen you wanting."

"That was one day."

"And one kiss."

Her heart dipped, scurrying for cover. There was something unsettling about the way he closed in, deceptively casual, carefully relentless.

"Want to try two, Carolina? You can prove me wrong once and for all."

Peering straight ahead and no higher, she watched the vein on the side of his throat beating. "I don't think I have to prove anything."

"But you want to. You want me to believe you're different from what everyone says."

"And what does everyone say?"

"That you're passionate. Strong willed. Loyal. And none too bright."

That made her look up.

He crooked a grin. "At least, not where love is concerned."

"Isn't hearsay evidence inadmissable?"

He nodded gravely. "I make sure my sources are reliable."

Then he leaned forward. Carolina leaned as far back as she could, but he wasn't reaching for her. A small square key clinked in a saucer on the tea tray. "Eve gave me that."

Gingerly, Carolina retrieved the key, rubbing it between her fingers. It was tarnished, thinly made, with two square teeth. Her blood ran cold. "Did she tell you what this was for?"

"Your diary."

"I burned it. You couldn't have read it."

"I wouldn't have. Did Eve?"

Carolina nodded.

"That doesn't sound like her."

"It wasn't. I was going through some difficult times, teenage years without Mom or my father. Gram was trying to understand. She said I kept too much inside." Actually, she'd said Carolina kept her passions hidden. Did she tell Brad that? Or had he guessed on his own?

"You asked me if she read it," Carolina stated. "That means she couldn't have told you what was in it."

"You'd make a good lawyer."

"And?"

"Now that I know she read it, I tend to believe the things she told me. That, and her raising you all your life, makes her a good judge of your character."

"On the basis of this?" Carolina tossed the key back in the saucer. "Flimsy evidence, counselor."

"There's more."

She paused, a shiver running through her like heat lightning.

"Ever hear of physical evidence?" He touched her. This time he wasn't asking, this time he knew. "That kiss said a lot."

"It said a wrung-out, emotionally fragile woman flung herself in the arms of the nearest man. I don't find that flattering to either one of us."

"You want to forget it?"

"Yes."

"Funny. I want to relive it."

He tugged her into his arms. This kiss was blunt, explicit, nothing like the one on the porch, which had been tender, comforting, had answered her needs. This one frankly answered needs all its own, outspoken in its expectations.

She yielded, but only to sensation. The emotions were too close to the surface, too jumbled, too uncontrollable to be unleashed. Two weeks ago he'd made her feel right, steadied. Now she felt like that damned bat, fluttering around near the ceiling, lost and desperate, a wild thing obeying instinct. And the instinct was to surrender.

He tore his mouth from hers. Her shoulders were clutched in his hands. She looked as shaken as he was. "Talk to me, 'Lina. It can be private or public, I don't care. I want to know who you are, how you feel. I want it from you, not every busybody in town."

He had to convince himself she was real, not the dream he'd been dreaming for years, not a phantom in his blood. Everyone saw how strong she was, how defiant. No one had seen the need—until Eve gave him the key. "I want to *know* you, Carolina."

There was a biblical connotation in there he sensed she didn't like. She eased her hands down his arms and pushed. He let her step back. "I think you should go."

Breathing hard, the white-knight part of him agreed. He wasn't going to rush her twice, even if her lips had confirmed what her mouth wouldn't utter. She wanted him. He could wait. "Meet me. In town. We'll have lunch."

"That's one way to get everyone talking."

"Dinner, then."

"Even better. How about meeting in your office? When we have *real* business to discuss?"

"They'll talk anyway. They already say I'm courting you."

"And I'm supposed to prove them right?"

From the way he peered at her, she was convinced she already had. A door in her heart, rusty and rarely ajar, creaked open. She'd asked him to listen—he had. But he expected her to keep giving, keep opening up. "Whatever Gram said—"

"Can't compare with what I feel. I know when something's ripe, Carolina. Like a peach. Juicy and ready."

Cupping the side of her neck with his palm, he ran his hand up over her collarbone, lightly, inch by inch, as if fighting the urge to slide it over her breast.

She shook her head, but it only played to the way he stroked her cheek. Breathing shallowly, insufficiently, she was breathless, dizzy. If she didn't say something, she was afraid she'd moan. "It's late."

"Talk to me, Carrie. What are you afraid of?"

"That you'll kiss me again." The faint blue vein on the side of her throat counted off the seconds under his thumb.

"Anything else?"

"That you won't."

He folded her to him as her arms went around his back. The crook of his elbow cradled the back of her neck. She leaned into it, forced gently back by the urgency of his mouth, seeking his taste before sense or defenses could get in their way.

His kiss was sweet and long, deep and revealing, insinuating every taboo act hidden away in darkness, every longing hour of loneliness they'd spent apart.

The next was like the night air. He molded his hand to her breast, the lace as scratchy to her sensitive nipple as his beard would be.

He would be like shadow, Carolina thought, studying the stubble hazing his cheeks. He'd be darkness and air.

Heavy, humid desire pooled inside her. She felt heated, weighted. She wanted to sink beneath him in feather beds, to rise, released from the past, from mistakes, from this prison of propriety she'd hidden behind so long. Maybe she wasn't like Gram or her mother, but there were times, needy times, when she wanted so badly to be.

"I came through that door tonight thinking you needed saving." His voice rustled through her hair, his harsh breath mimicking hers. "You do, don't you?"

But there were other doors, not so easily opened. And there was something she had to ask, nagging at the edge of her mind like the squeak of that bat dragging her out of her dream, the creak of a hinge. "The door."

"No one will come in. Except maybe me." His tone made her tremble.

"But how?"

"Just you wait," he said with a chuckle.

She turned her face, thwarting his next kiss. "I meant, how did you get in?"

"I have a key. Eve gave it to me in case she locked herself out. How was I to know you'd need saving so soon?" He ducked his head, his lips skimming her neck. His beard sizzled against the satiny fabric. "And that you'd be wearing this."

Even with her eyes closed, Carolina sensed the smile on his wide mouth as he trailed a line of kisses over a shoulder now bare. "But—"

"I'm renting the cottage."

"Henry's cottage?"

"He moved into town."

"You didn't tell me."

"Anyone in town could have. All you had to do was ask."

He had her there. Asking around would have meant showing an interest, and she'd been so swift to discourage every offer of gossip about Brad Lavalier.

"It's no secret," he said.

Oh, dear Lord. Carolina moaned. The handsome-est, single-est, most available man in Grelickville, and they were living out there alone. No wonder people thought they were—

Blood flushed her cheeks, passion converted to heat, flustered into action. Her loosened robe fluttered wildly as she frantically tossed cups and spoons on the tea tray. "You've got to go."

"I will when you simmer down."

"You can't live here."

"I'm not. Yet."

She almost threw the lukewarm tea at him. "I mean there. You've been encouraging them, haven't you? Letting people think you come over here in the evening."

He drawled out his disappointment. "Carolina, I wouldn't."

"Go out the back. That way no one will see you. Go on. Git!"

He sighed as he headed down the hall toward the kitchen door and the back porch. "Who said a minute ago she'd learned to live with what people thought?"

Waking the next morning to the sound of a Sunday revival service, Carolina realized she must have gotten some sleep. Thankfully it had been a cool night.

She'd sat up for hours, alternately denouncing Brad Lavalier, her own weakness, and Gram's mischief-making plans. Carolina was firmly ensconced in this house for a year, and the only lawyer she'd dared confide to was Brad Lavalier.

"What do you bet his lease is for one year?" She muttered a curse the room had probably never heard.

As if his living out back wasn't bad enough, his ghost dawdled throughout the house as she marched downstairs for breakfast. She could shake curtains to dislodge any leftover bats, but she couldn't dislodge the subtle whiff of his cologne, the teacup he'd left on an end table. She'd missed it in her hurry to clean away every trace of him the previous night. The spot on the rug where they'd stood wasn't going away either. Or the sensation of being wrapped in his arms.

She scowled. "Think you convinced him Gram was wrong?"

He probably now believed in the Palmette Curse as surely as some people stayed home on Friday the thirteenth.

Grinding her teeth, she trudged into the kitchen. Okay, so she glanced out the screen door first, catching no sign of life at the cottage. Was there anything wrong with that? She'd been convinced for three weeks it was empty. How could she have suspected he lived there?

"The man must be burrowed in there like a mole. Emerging only to rush in my front door at the first peep from me."

She ripped apart an orange over the sink, waiting for her coffee to boil.

Brad would've been only to happy to help Gram when she was locked out, to close her windows, listen to her stories, kiss her granddaughter senseless.

"Bah!" Carolina snapped at the toast as it popped. A puddle of black coffee sloshed onto the counter as she poured.

There was only one answer to this arrangement. Ignore it. Same thing for those kisses. Don the armor as if the battle had never happened, as if no ground had been surrendered. As if she'd actually slept through the night.

"You have to get back that key."

She took a moment to think, interrupted by the echo of his parting shot as he'd disappeared into the darkness off the back porch.

"Next time I want in, Carolina, you'll be letting me."

"Thumbtacks!" Carolina huffed, borrowing an old favorite of Gram's. She'd keep busy. She'd work. She wouldn't think of keys or curses or Brad Lavalier, Esquire.

Carolina stared off into the amber of her computer

screen as she sat down to work in the dining room. Ripe. The word flashed through her as she sank her teeth into an orange section. Juicy.

"Bushwa." If she couldn't get the man out of her head to stay, she'd have to admit Gram was right. She was every bit as foolish as her choices, as headstrong and heart-weak as every other Palmette.

"Self-knowledge is the first step to self-control," she murmured. This was one Palmette who wasn't living up to, or down to, the family reputation.

She would not melt. She would not surrender her life to a husband on a pedestal. And she *would not* be the talk of Grelickville!

Four hours later, when the brass knocker pounded against the door, she was prepared to confront Godzilla himself. Just as soon as she wiped spilled coffee off a folder, she'd march down that hall and demand the key, and her hands would *not* shake when he handed it over.

So what if she was wearing little more than a tank top and a shapeless cotton dress that hung loosely to her shins? When a woman had willpower, a power suit wasn't necessary. She wasn't expecting company, and it was too hot for nylons, so why should her toes feel so naked?

For a second, the blurry silhouette outside the beveled glass door had Carolina wondering if sleepless nights and enough coffee produced hallucinations. To her knowledge, mirages didn't come dressed in large, flower-bedecked hats. She opened the door.

"Dotty!" Carolina threw her arms around the old woman in sheer relief.

Dotty Willis, Gram's cook and maid of thirty years, eased out of the embrace. "Don't be clinging all over me, child, it's hot as a fresh-baked pie out here." She stepped into the foyer. "You been getting too much sun, 'Lina?" She touched Carolina's cheek.

Not too much sun, Carolina thought, remembering another touch, too much heat. "But this isn't your day."

"Land sakes, no. And I wouldn't be in this outfit to clean, neither." Dotty tried to indicate her dress, a flowery affair with a magnolia pinned to the bosom. The motion was complicated by a casserole dish in her hands. "Wanted to drop in afore you started your Sunday dinner."

Since Carolina's dinner consisted of whatever was in the freezer, she thanked Dotty graciously and followed her into the kitchen, trailing the scent of shrimp casserole.

Dotty lit the old oven with a match. "One and a half hours, no more, or you'll dry it out. Sprinkle some shoestring potatoes on top when it's done." She reached for a hot pad that wasn't there, frowned, and found one in a drawer.

"Yes'm," Carolina obediently replied. If Dotty glanced in the cupboards, she'd find Carolina lacking shoestring potatoes too. "But you're not going so soon?"

"Actually, I was hoping you and I could have a talk, Care-line."

The pronunciation made Carolina feel ten years old. "I'd love to, Dotty. Let me turn off my computer."

Dotty was already checking the contents of the refrigerator. "You go on ahead. Looks like I've got plenty to do in here."

When Carolina returned, Dotty set an iced tea in front of her. It was useless to fuss. She'd be waited on no end and hushed if she tried anything more than sitting and saying thank you.

"Been over to the reverend's service this mornin'," the older woman began. "He's been wanting me to invest in this church he *sez* he's planning on building."

"And?"

"I wanted your opinion. You always was a bright one."

Except where men were concerned, Carolina thought. "Investing is different from donating, Dotty. Has he promised you any kind of return?"

"No. But he was at the will reading; he knows how much your Gram left me. Anyhow, I went to see that young attorney about it too."

"Brad?"

"What do you think of him, child?"

"I couldn't rightly say."

"He's a fine, handsome young man."

"Is that what you want my opinion on?"

"Closemouthed as ever." Dotty shook her head, chuckling and humming as she puttered with the salad fixings.

"What advice did he give you?" Carolina asked, feeling a trifle perturbed. Brad wasn't the only one who acted as if he saw right through her.

"He says what I do with my money's up to me and not to be pressured by anybody."

"That's very sensible." Sensible was the last thing Carolina felt when his name was mentioned. Part of her rebelled at thinking any good of him at all. He'd waltzed into her house with his own key and kissed her as if, as if—

She jumped when the teapot whistled.

"Go easy, child. I'm just brewing up more tea."

Tea. It was better than the third degree and a white-hot spotlight. She remembered Brad's comment and knew she was in for expert questioning.

Dotty stepped on the metal trash-can pedal and tossed in the soggy tea bags.

Carolina's hopes that some company would take her mind off Brad went the same route. Maybe if she limited their conversation to business . . . "Did he have any other suggestions?"

"He said Sunday might be a good day to talk to you

about it. You work too hard during the week, he says."

Of course, what she'd been working on was avoiding him whenever possible.

"So what do I do about the Reverend Shepherd and this special seat in heaven he's offering?"

Carolina got up and gave Dotty a hug. "Let's make sure you're looked after in the here and now. We'll go over the portfolio options my firm offers. My computer's in the dining room."

"Hush, child, the kitchen's good enough for me. I just need your brains and common sense." Dotty seated herself with a huff and a whiff of perfume, fanning herself with a napkin while Carolina briefly outlined various mutual funds.

Dotty listened carefully. "Care-line, is this what you recommend?"

"Yes ma'am. That would be a very sound invest-ment plan."

"And what about this Lavalier fellow?"

"What about him?"

"You sleeping with him yet?"

Six

Carolina nearly choked on her iced tea. She pulled her mouth into a tight frown. "I don't know what rumors are going around, but I'd appreciate it if you'd set people straight. I really don't see—"

"Child, you don't sleep with that man, and you don't see anything a'tall. He's hungry for you."

Great, she was back to being a juicy peach. She shut a manila folder and began collecting her brochures. "Dotty, I don't want to talk about this."

"You know your grandmother rented him Henry Soapkins's place out back."

"I do, but there's been nothing untoward about the arrangement, I assure you." Unfortunately, the color in her cheeks was warmer than the chilliness of her words.

And Dotty was no dummy. "I can see that. Explain it to me again."

"Dotty."

"Them high-security bonds. How the quarterly yield adds to the principal."

The woman struck like a water snake and retreated like a sleeping opossum.

Carolina bit her tongue. "Bonds." Her emotions a swamp of sleeplessness and restlessness, she didn't give a damn about Class A bonds *or* penny stocks. She explained them patiently anyway.

Dotty spoke up again. "I jus' don't understand it."

"I can go over it again."

"I mean, whatever you're holdin' against the man."

Carolina sighed. "I don't hold anything against him." Not that she hadn't dreamed of his holding her.

"Child, he was as faithful and friendly to your Gram as anyone could be. He'd come by here and help out, never in too much hurry to chat."

That was Brad all right. Taking things as they came, slow, deliberate. Luxuriating, relishing.

It was this atmosphere. It slowed a person down. Made them too aware, too full of feeling and lazy, erotic dreams.

And there wasn't anything particularly wrong with the man. Dotty was right there. He cared. He came around. He listened. Lord, did he listen.

Up North she would have sold her soul to find a man like him. Why run from him? Good question, she thought. Why let fears she thought she'd left behind six years ago color her life now?

Because running away never solved anything. As long as she was in Grelickville, she'd be talked about. She either lived like a nun or risked scandal. Weren't there any other choices?

"He may not have the big practice," Dotty was saying, "but don't be fooled. That young man is sharp as a tack in a brand new whitewall. Besides, to hear Mizz Palmette tell it, you're doing all right for yourself moneywise."

"I'm doing fine." If you considered a condo, a car, and a portfolio of one's own, success. Just about everyone she knew did.

"What do you think your Gram would advise you on this one?"

Carolina rolled her eyes. "'Get yourself a man. You got nothing without love.'"

Both women laughed, although Carolina suspected

for different reasons. "A man isn't the answer to everything, Dotty."

"No, but he can make a lot of things right that's wrong. Fill up a lot of empty places."

Carolina crossed to the sink and rinsed her glass with a gush of water, only to remember Brad drinking from the fountain in the mausoleum, wiping water from his lips with the back of his hand. Was there any way she'd get him off her mind? "When did Gram get these new faucets?" It was an innocuous enough question.

"Young Lavalier. He brought 'em around. Installed 'em one afternoon with Henry."

Carolina's breathy sigh turned into a laugh. Brad might as well walk through the door and have a seat; he couldn't be any more central to the conversation. The man was as pervasive as humidity in July.

A floorboard squeaked on the back porch and both women turned as the screen door opened.

"Afternoon, ladies." Brad touched a finger to his forehead in a courtly salute.

Carolina's heart tumbled in her chest like ice in a tall glass.

Yes, she realized. Gram would want her to have just such a man. He was charming when she wanted remote, respectful of everything but her wish to be left alone, easy and ingratiating when she wanted businesslike and distant. He knew things about her only her nearest and dearest could have told—and things only a man who kissed the way he did, who watched her the way he did, could find out.

He was handsome as the devil, too, conjuring up desires she'd never openly acknowledged, needs that ran perilously close to longings.

It had to be the heat.

And the way he smiled.

"Afternoon," Carolina replied.

"Sleep late?" he asked.

"I slept just fine, thank you." A full three hours, at

least. Not that her sleeping arrangements were any business of his. "Dotty, I'd like you to take those notes home and read them over. Ask the brokers in town if you want a second opinion."

"Good advice," Brad allowed. "Always trust a person who's open to a second opinion. Or a second chance."

Carolina gave him a tight smile but finished with Dotty first. "You want to be very careful when investing a good portion of what you'll be living on. We can't always rely on the church."

"I've always said the Lord will provide."

"But not always in good hard cash," Brad interjected with a grin.

He was as charming and alluring as a daybed tucked into a private corner, a blatant invitation to come lie down. So why couldn't she ignore her quicksilver sensations when he was around, the kind a needier woman might call eagerness?

His clothes were sun warmed, beginning to wrinkle. She could almost feel the heat radiating off him and guessed he'd walked up from the cottage, suit coat hitched over his shoulder. When he leaned against the refrigerator, it was she who felt off-kilter.

Dotty broke the silence by getting to her feet. "You look like a fella who'd appreciate an iced tea."

Brad licked his parched lips and came all the way into the room. "Much obliged, Dotty. 'Lina." He nodded by way of a more formal greeting as he took a seat.

She flushed at the intentional intimacy. "Most people call me Carolina."

"Until they know you better," Dotty corrected.

"That's kind of what I had in mind." Brad grinned.

Carolina shivered, a wave of cold air from the freezer touching her as Dotty got out more ice. She listened to the tea pour, heard the cubes crack. She was intently aware of everything in the kitchen, from the smell of shrimp casserole to the worn patches in the linoleum to Dotty's humming. All of it registered;

all of it distracted; none of it stopped her from staring into Brad's eyes.

"You join us for supper now," Dotty commanded.

"I was kind of hoping you'd invite me," he replied, voice low. "I've been wanting to join y'all for a while now." He pushed out a kitchen chair with the toe of his shoe. "Have yourself a seat, Carolina."

She hesitated. He shrugged as if there were no hurry. She knew he thought her pace too northern. But down there haste deserted her, replaced by a desire to savor the moment, to drawl out a reply, to sink lazily into that chair and prove to him she wasn't normally so skittish.

" 'Lina? Ain't you going to thank the gentleman?"

Carolina's rear end hit the kitchen chair with a thump. "Thank you kindly."

"She's getting her accent back, notice?" Brad said to Dotty.

"Ah did. Sounds like it ought. Here, you get some of this into you."

Brad took a long swallow of tea, licking his lips and grinning like an old polecat.

Carolina reminded herself cats were lazy, too, until they spotted their prey and pounced.

"Actually," he began, "I stopped by to invite Ms. Palmette to visit me for lunch sometime next week."

Carolina laughed and shook her head. If he thought he was going to sucker her into saying yes merely because they had an audience . . . "I think someone's been out in the sun too long, Dotty."

"Think someone just asked you out on a date, young lady," she replied sharply.

Carolina grimaced.

Brad chuckled, encouraged to have found an ally. "It's a fine eating establishment, Giroux's, just this side of McMichael's Shoes."

"Where the old hardware store used to be."

"Thank you, Dotty, I know it."

"I'd appreciate the opportunity to sit a spell and talk," he added.

An opening occurred to Carolina, and she switched subjects as smoothly as a locomotive on a worn track. "You're right, we should talk."

Brad leaned back, one foot almost astride hers as he stretched his long legs under the table. He tucked a thumb in a belt loop. "Looks like I got lucky, Dotty."

"What better way to show the reverend we're united against him?" Carolina stated firmly. "The more pressure we put on him, the faster we'll scare him off that land."

Dotty grunted as if she'd just heard some nonsense that didn't deserve comment. "You two want salad?"

"I 'spect so," Brad said, his gaze never leaving Carolina's.

She fought a tight sensation in her throat by sipping her water. "You *are* looking into Shepherd's background, aren't you?"

He nodded. "The longer I look, the longer it seems to take."

She wasn't sure he meant Shepherd's case or her eyes. Too many thoughts clogged her brain, careening off sensations. She watched him handling his glass, his long fingers curving around it, the pad of a thumb connecting dots of moisture. Moisture of a different sort glistened on her skin.

Wordlessly, he stated his terms. He'd help her catch Shepherd, but she'd have to stick around while he did—and resist Brad Lavalier to the best of her ability.

Resist him she would.

Brad grinned, admiring the way she drew her shoulders back when she was cornered—cornered, not beaten. The woman had enough pride to weather any scandal, but she didn't seem to know it, or that her knight in armor was right there—she just had to hop up on the horse with him.

Watching Dotty bustle down the hallway, he was

about to put some of that into words. Instead he said, "You look tired."

"I haven't been sleeping well. The heat."

He nodded in answer. He'd seen her on the balcony, seeking relief, seeking something. He, too, knew how prolonged the sultry hours after midnight could be, how tardy the dawn. He knew what she'd dreamt when sleep came at last; he'd dreamed it too.

"I'll be going now," Dotty announced, startling them both. "Soon as the water's boiling, you drop in those beans."

"You're not staying for supper?" Carolina rose from her chair.

"Thought you could use some good cooking. Jus' take it out of the oven when you're ready." She plopped on her flowered hat. "You don't need my help for the next part."

Carolina ignored Brad's grin as they escorted Dotty to the door. Out on the lawn, they watched her drive away in a massive old Plymouth, puffs of gray smoke chugging from the exhaust like the heavy black clouds gathering over the flat land.

As the storm moved along the horizon, Carolina felt a queer kind of quivering in her limbs, like the leaves on the trees anticipating thunder. They were alone. She strode to the foot of the front porch, searching for something to say. "Do you always invite yourself to supper?"

"I saw we'd have a chaperon and thought I'd stop by. That is what you wanted, isn't it? Keeping this respectable?"

"We don't have one now. Besides, everyone knows you live out here. Dotty said as much."

"Gossip doesn't have to hurt."

"Doesn't it? I've been the butt end of it since I was nothing more than my mother's reason for leaving town." She stopped right there, hugging her arms around herself, aware of how flimsy her dress was— her dress and her excuses. That's what running had done for her. She'd returned to confront everything all over again. But things that might have been valid to a twenty-year-old girl wilted when a woman leaned on them for support, seeking an excuse to turn a man away.

"'Everyone does it and anything goes and nobody minds—'"

"'—as long as everybody knows.'" He completed the children's rhyme with her. "Word gets around."

"And the word was out on me a long time ago."

But did it matter? She wasn't that girl anymore, why worry about her spotless reputation? Because it mattered so much once. Reevaluation wasn't easy. Standing near Brad Lavalier wasn't any easier. She reached for the words to explain to them both why it would be better if he left.

"I'm not apologizing for things that happened before I was born, but I don't treasure living up to whatever picture people have of me. I need to know there's some part of me that isn't up for public discussion. Do you understand?"

"I understand I have to get to know you before I can make any claims, Carolina. I tried to tell you that last night."

He placed a foot on the bottom step, slacks taut, leg muscles outlined. She felt the heat of him, the stirring of a breeze pushed by the storm. He bent like a willow to be closer, body lean and sinewy.

"I've heard the legend, tell me about the woman."

She waved a strand of hair away with his words. "Legend about says it."

"And you? What do you want? What do you like?"

What did she like? The sound of his voice. The easiness about him that said he didn't judge anyone too fast; she'd felt judged all her life. The compelling glint in his eye that urged her to him.

"Did you like that kiss last night? I was up thinking about it a long time."

Why'd he have to remind her? "Yes," she said, "so was I. You never did give me the house key."

Pursing his lips, he studied the stairs a moment. "You want it?"

Those three words could apply to a lot of things. "The key, please."

He sunk a hand into his pocket and fished out a jangling ring. "It's all yours."

She wasn't about to slip that ring off his finger. "Just the front door key, please."

He flipped one over, then another. "What about the Oldsmobile? Eve liked me to start it up sometimes, take it out on the highway. Every engine needs to burn hot now and then to keep it from seizing up." He handed her the first key. "When do you burn, Carolina?"

She glared at him. "When I don't get my way. The house key, please."

He grinned at her spirit. "Want one to the cottage? A landlady needs a key."

She'd been ready to turn it down until he put it that way. "I guess—all right. Just in case I have to get in."

The keys were warm from being in his pocket, their teeth pricked her palm as he closed his hand around hers. Electricity crackled in the air.

"They're all yours, 'Lina."

He touched a thumb to the dark circle under one of her eyes. She flinched. So did he, inside. "If there's anytime you can't sleep, you want to come down to me . . ."

She had to speak, to stall this storm, stem the feelings gathering like a tide about to hit shore. "I wouldn't presume—"

"I'd be awake. I usually am. Especially when I think you're having the same problem."

He was her problem. Him and these feelings that the sanest, surest Palmette wasn't supposed to have. Her emotions swirled like gusts of wind, tugging at the hem of her dress, kiting it in and out between her legs. "What do you want?"

"You," he replied, his voice a little rough.

"And?"

"I think you're old enough to figure out the rest. I want the woman I'm looking at. Not a reputation, not a family line. I want you clear as day and shiny as the stars at night."

His voice was a magnetic murmur, climbing slow and steady along her nerve endings.

"I don't want you standing on that balcony alone, Carolina. I want to be there with you."

"The balcony?" she echoed softly.

He wanted her to realize he'd been there, had already seen. It wasn't a question of what Eve said, or the people in town. He'd kissed her, held her, seen her in suits and silk robes and considerably less. He'd seen the Carolina no one else saw, the one who let down her hair and stood in the sultry swelter of the night, face upturned to the stars, letting the air caress her like a lover. Sensual, passionate, a woman with no shame.

He loved what he'd seen with his own two eyes, not what others had told him. Wasn't that what she wanted to hear?

Apparently not. She howled as if he'd just thrown cold water on her.

"You've been watching me!"

"There are nights I can't sleep either, 'Lina."

"But there's been no light, no car—" she sputtered.

"There've been too many cars, all of them from the revival. You probably didn't hear mine."

"And you park it out back behind the cottage like Henry did his!"

"The garage is for you."

"And the cottage for you and your—your ringside seat. For all I know you probably look forward to seeing me naked!"

He clenched his jaw. "Now that I won't deny."

"That does it. You're evicted. There's no way you can live out there."

"I've got a year left on my lease."

"Don't you trade legalities with me," she shouted, waving a shaking finger at him. "I could have you arrested!"

With Carolina as judge and jury, he already heard the gavel pounding out his guilty sentence. "You won't," he replied evenly.

"Won't I?"

"Think of the scandal."

He hit her with another gallon of cold water. Why didn't he just fetch a bucket? he wondered with a smile.

"*That* is low," she snarled, eyes flashing. He knew she'd die rather than give people in town more to talk about.

"Question is," he said, "if I'm not moving, how long will you be staying?"

"If I leave, the house reverts to the reverend, and you know it. Or was that Gram's plan all along? To trap me here with a Peeping Tom?"

She flung off any defense he was brazen enough to muster. "Isn't this neat?" she muttered. "Me here for a year, and you out back with your lease. And your telescope."

He touched her arm. "All a man has to do is look."

"Don't you dare blame this on me. I never knew you were there."

"But I know you. The real you. Isn't that what you're afraid of? That some man will see the passion? Touch it off like a fuse just by doing this?"

He hauled her into his arms, his kiss hard and fast. His kiss, not theirs. The night before he'd held a wanton, now he held a statue.

His lips were scant inches from hers when he spoke again. "I see you, Carolina. You can hide from every busybody in town, but not from me. Not from a man who wants you."

"Oh no?" She wriggled out of his grasp, stalking across the porch. A crack of thunder answered the resounding slap of the screen as she ducked inside.

"Way to go, Lavalier." Why was it a man who had all the time in the world for other things always moved too fast for this woman?

"Probably because he's a lovesick fool," he muttered.

Brad plunged his hands in his pockets and stood staring at her door. He could simply wait her out, but he suspected his chances were better of getting struck by lightning. Or he could walk through that door, take her in his arms and . . .

"Conan the Barbarian goes courting."

He scuffed a shoe across the gravel. It crunched with a chalky screech, like the pots and pans she was banging together in there. A door slammed inside.

It echoed in Brad.

For the last ten nights he'd waited at his window, lights out, drink in hand, a fire brewing in his gut as he'd watched his dream become a walking reality. On four nights she'd appeared, glistening from her shower, arms lifted, elbows bent, hands lost in her own hair, uninhibited in the inky dark.

At her first shriek last night, he'd run to the house, hell-bent and clammy with sweat. The relief he'd felt when her screams proved groundless had nearly knocked him off his feet.

How many ways did he want to save the woman? he wondered. Could he save her from her stubborn pride? From the neediness he alone saw? "Carolina, you're wanting, honey. Let me be there," he said aloud.

Thunder grumbled.

The screen cracked open. She had a dustpan in her hand, and the broom, her weapon of choice.

"What are you doing out there? I said git." She might just as well have shooed a cat in heat. He stood immobile at the edge of the drive.

"I didn't figure we were done yet," he replied.

"We were done the first time you spied on me."

He shrugged. "Then we start over."

Her mouth fell open. "Get out of here before half the neighborhood sees you mooning around like some Romeo. Shoo."

He shook his head mournfully. "No can do, 'Lina."

"And don't call me that."

"I've waited a long time, I can wait a while longer."

"If you lift your head up you can drown, too, turkey." She slammed the door on his laughter as the first fat raindrops splattered on the lawn.

A drop fell, a ticking sounded on the porch roof, then a clatter on the gravel. At the first thunderclap, the clouds tore open and the deluge hit.

Seven

Ten minutes later, a car drove by on the rutted road, wipers slapping, horn honking. Carolina came to the door and waved as perkily as she could. "What are they gonna think, you standing out here in the rain?"

"Anything they want."

"If I get you an umbrella, will you go home?"

He shrugged, but she took it as a yes. Old boots flew as she ferreted out a musty black umbrella from the hall wardrobe. Marching onto the porch, she shoved it at him point first. "Here."

He acknowledged her silent *En garde.*

One step at a time, he ascended the stairs, the back of his hand pushing the tip aside. He stopped close enough for her to smell the mint on his breath, the soaked clothes. She felt weak and tense at the same time, alert and alive. Also indignant and supremely self-righteous about it. "I don't see where you get off spying on a woman who thinks she's alone."

"She needs to know she doesn't have to be."

"Says who?"

"You. Your lips when I kiss you. Your eyes. They never said you didn't want me."

They would have if he hadn't touched her first. His

hand on her arm silenced her, robbed her of breath. How silly, she thought, it was only her arm. His thumb rested in the crook of her elbow. Should that make her shake like a tree limb?

He turned her hand, studied the fine blue lines on the inside of her wrist. She marveled at how sensitive the skin there was and went weak. He wasn't supposed to be kissing it. "What exactly do you think you're doing?"

"Exactly?" He shook his head, unable to explain. "I can't put this part in writing, 'Lina. I think it comes under the heading of mutual consent."

Her pulse rumbled so unsteadily, she couldn't distinguish it from the thunder. "Is it?" She meant, is it mutual? It was important that she know she wasn't the only one coming undone.

She withdrew her arm, unconsciously wiping her wrist against her dress. It wasn't disgust that made her do it, far from it. It was the imprint of his lips. She tried to laugh. "I think you've been up one too many nights staring at the stars."

"It's been a mighty pretty sight."

She didn't tremble at the naked appreciation in his eyes. Not outwardly.

The rain poured down, splashing on the overhanging dogwood, tapping the flowering vines creeping up the side of the house, unleashing their extravagant, profligate fragrance.

"I need my privacy." Her voice was a whispered plea.

"If you let me be part of it."

He already was—in her house, in her dreams, inside her defenses and luring her ever farther into the open. She clenched her hand; he opened it with his tongue, planting kisses in the soft center.

Another car went by. She almost forgot to care. She pulled back her hand. "I think you should go."

Brad could wait out stubbornness, even pride, but not the trace of fear in her eyes, the vulnerability that told him she wanted him as much as he wanted her.

She wasn't ready to take that last step. He could push her over it—if he was bastard enough to try.

He wouldn't; the honorable part of him reared its trusty head. "Guess the road to hell is paved with good intentions." He stepped off the porch and into the rain. "Call me when you're in the mood for flames."

Strolling around the house, he sidestepped a gush of water running off a downspout. He was soaked anyway, his clothes sticking to him everywhere.

"Brad!" Carolina popped open the umbrella and ran after him. When he turned, she stopped so fast, she skidded on the sodden grass and let out a little yelp.

The rain hung like a beaded curtain between them.

"You're going to catch your death if you don't move a little faster," she said, faintly breathless.

"Are you suggesting I get out of these clothes?" He spread his hands wide, teasing her with a grin that never made it into his eyes.

The man couldn't possibly think she'd rush into those arms, could he? Not after he'd invaded her life, asking after her, spying on her, breaching her defenses with the tenderest of kisses, getting her to unburden her heart while he listened patiently, caringly, absolutely unforgivably. He was outrageous, audacious—and utterly sweet. He was mad if he thought she'd forgive him.

He was also apparently willing to ruin a perfectly good suit while standing in the rain. It was beyond her comprehension how a man managed to be as sexy as a swashbuckling hero when by all accounts he should've looked like a drowned rat. "Lavalier?"

"Yes, Carolina?"

"Anyone ever tell you you need a full-time caretaker?"

"Why, 'Lina. You can take care of me anytime, sugar."

She huffed in a passable imitation of Dotty. "I'm walking you back to your cottage under this umbrella, you got that? No funny stuff. And *no* kissing."

And no telling exactly when her heart had gone out to him, or when exactly she'd ever get it back.

"Come on. You'll catch pneumonia, and then who'll I use for legal advice?" She pursed her lips firmly and kept her gaze forward.

"Yes, Carolina," he murmured, ducking his head under the umbrella and falling into step.

The runoff dribbling down his back didn't bother him much at all. He wondered if the cloudburst pelted her bare legs the way it did his slacks. The rain was warm, his clothes cold, his flesh heating up nicely with her beside him. He closed his fingers around hers on the umbrella handle. She was going to walk him to his door, deposit him like some overnight delivery, then leave.

Unless he came up with a better alternative.

"I didn't spy on you," he insisted.

"Then who was it?"

"You and me both. We've been there already, Carolina. In my dreams. In yours. Tell me that isn't true."

She couldn't. A drop of rain cascaded down her back like a fingertip tracing her spine, and she straightened. "You invaded my privacy." He was doing it again, making her want, making her ache. "My life isn't open to public discussion."

"This is private as can be, Carolina. It has nothing to do with the town or curses or where I live. It's me wanting you, that's all. I want the woman I see when I do this."

He kissed her, wrapping his arms around her waist, lifting her clear off her feet and turning them three hundred and sixty degrees, taking her around the world and back again. The umbrella spun like a black mushroom. When he was done, when he considered her thoroughly, utterly, and emphatically kissed, he set her down.

She let out a tiny gasp when her feet hit the grass and she realized she'd lost a sandal.

He watched her eyes flutter shut as his mouth met hers, her body aligned with his perfectly, if vertically. "Take off the other one," he said.

She complied, bumping his thigh with hers as she kicked it off. Grass prickled between her toes. It was the only sensation that permeated her woozy senses. The mud came next, squishy and forbidden and sensuous. Where was sensible, responsible Carolina now? she wondered.

She held on to him, balancing while she looked down at a grimy sole. "I can't believe I'm playing in mud puddles. This is crazy."

"As bad as chasing bats with broom handles?"

"As bad as waiting for some woman to come along you've only seen in pictures?"

He shrugged, unoffended. "She did, didn't she?"

He kissed her. And kissed her. Her toes suddenly became the least of her problems. In the great scheme of things, breathing, keeping her knees from buckling, and remembering her own name loomed infinitely larger.

The breeze eddied about them, moving the humidity around. Then he hit the catch and the umbrella collapsed. Carolina gasped as the rain hit her.

Rain warm as tears, sweet as honey, drenched everything, washing away indecision, leaving a rainbow of wonder in its place. A rich dampness, thick and moist as spring, saturated the air. The rain never stopped. And his kisses were just beginning.

Her cotton dress felt transparent, slicked against every curve and womanly mound. Her hair was plastered to her forehead. His tongue touched one droplet, his lips another. Nectar.

Then his mouth found her ear, his hands everything else. Breasts, wrists, the flare of her hips, the moistness between her legs.

"Stay with me, sugar."

Consent. It had seemed so complicated the night before. Now it was only a matter of reaching for him, making sure her arms didn't slip from around his neck, her mouth returned every seeking kiss. He wanted her there, with him step by step. She could love a man like him. One who possessed such tenderness, such fire.

A ragged breath escaped him as her hands scanned the ridges of his ribs, her thumbs scaling the peaks of taut nipples.

Where had her struggle gone? Her resistance? It had been washed away.

The man cared, and, shielded by the house from prying eyes, she wanted to show him she could too. She wanted to explore the passion she'd denied herself all her life.

"Funny," she said, her cheek against his.

Impatiently, he slicked wet hair off his forehead. A drop ran down the inside of his collar and down his back, sizzling as it went. "What is?"

"I've pictured you in a shower practically since we met."

Brad let that one rocket through him. He knew he hadn't been the only one dreaming.

"What have you pictured?" she asked him.

His voice was gritty, his throat tight. "You on the balcony."

"But that was real."

"Not the part where you tell me how much you want me."

She took his tongue in her mouth, exploring, penetrating. Then she coaxed his lips closed with her fingertips, gently, firmly.

"What is it?" he asked.

"*Too much.*" She wanted this too much. "I've waited so long for someone to come along the way Gram said he would. Wondering if I could ever love the way they did."

"Can you?"

"I don't know." She experienced one last shiver of doubt.

The Publisher of Loveswept® Romances invites you to:

CLAIM A FREE EXCLUSIVE ROMANCE

Lift Here

...PLUS SIX ROMANCES RISK FREE

6 ROMANCES RISK FREE

NO OBLIGATION TO BUY!

THE FREE GIFT IS YOURS TO KEEP

Detach and affix this stamp to the postage-paid reply card — and mail at once!

SEE DETAILS INSIDE ▶

YOU GET SIX
ROMANCES RISK FREE...
Plus AN EXCLUSIVE TITLE FREE!

- -

Loveswept Romances

He touched her cheek. "You're more like them than you know. I think that's what Eve found out in your diary. You wouldn't believe her."

"But you did."

"After I kissed you."

"I still don't know."

"Want to find out?"

He stroked her black, shining hair, her pebbled breast. Wet fabric slapped as he drew her dress up her thigh. "The porch." He nodded in that direction in case the words hadn't come out.

An old refrigerator hunched under the sagging roof, its sidekick a farmer's old milk churn and a barrel precipitously overgrown with flowers. A white wicker settee looked inviting with one lone cushion of blue flowered chintz. It was enough for a man and a woman to lie down on.

Her summer dress had buttons all the way down the front, frustrating little things, mother-of-pearl and slippery as the sea. He could've tugged it over her head, but he stubbornly undid each one. He parted it when he reached her waist, studying the white tank top, the dark olive skin beside it, the darker aureoles beneath.

Carolina took a deep breath and unbuttoned, unbuckled him in return, peeling his shirt away from the skin it clung to. Touching. Tasting.

The world tilted and the settee creaked beneath them. Their weight made it lurch precariously.

She laughed breathlessly. "I don't know if this will hold us."

He kicked an armrest. "People were a lot smaller in those days."

A moment passed as they stared into each other's eyes, listening to the rain pummel the ground.

She glanced in the direction of the cottage. "Hard to see with this monsoon."

But visible all the same. "This is still a little public," he said.

She nodded.

He helped her up. "You go first," he said, tipping his head toward the back door. "Call me when you're toweled off."

He'd said the next time she'd let him in. Carolina knew he was right. She stood, legs wobbly, resolve firm, and walked to the door.

Brad listened to the kitchen screen bang shut, her steps padding wetly on the linoleum. He knew when she got to the hallway runner he wouldn't hear her.

He wouldn't hear her climb the stairs either, or enter her bedroom, or run a fast warm shower.

He thought of fluffy towels, feather beds. Willing women.

He thought of Carolina and how many times he'd told himself not to rush it. "How many times are you going to tell yourself it's okay because she said yes?" he asked himself grimly.

She'd kicked him off the front porch not fifteen minutes before. From there to passion wasn't that big a step, not with a hot-blooded woman. Not with a needy one.

She'd said yes.

But only because he'd gotten her too fired up to say no.

Her passion was the key. He'd chased it, appealed to it, nurtured it, waited for it in the rain. He'd led her slowly up those steps and laid her slowly down. He'd made sure every step of the way she'd had a choice. As long as that choice was yes.

They both knew they were about to make love.

Only he knew what a mistake it would be.

Carolina wrapped the satin robe around her, forgoing the nightgown that went with it. She turned down the sheets. She waited for his footstep on the stairs. The rain had stopped, drips and drops punctuating the afternoon stillness. The lavish aroma of lush dark places, verdant and green, wafted through the open balcony doors.

Left alone, doubts had a way of multiplying, doubts that melted in his arms. So she went looking, eager to be with him, again, to be sure. She would open the door, just as he said. This time she'd invite him in.

But the back porch was empty. He was gone.

Monday was hot and dry, and Carolina had too many clothes on. The day before she'd been naked, cool, and wet, flushed and feverish in Brad's arms.

Carolina rearranged herself in the vinyl booth of Giroux's Diner and stared out at heat waves baking the asphalt.

"Hot again," Charlene, the waitress, said.

"Yes."

"Good and cool last night. Sleepin' weather."

"Yes, yes it was." Ice water bounded past the lump in Carolina's throat. She felt it all the way down.

When she woke that morning she'd almost convinced herself it was all a dream, the kind that left you achy and strangely wanting. Until reality crossed the street toward the restaurant in the form of Brad Lavalier, walking with an undeniable bounce in his step.

Carolina's heart did a swan dive, the air in her lungs felt musty and creaky as from an old air conditioner. She'd almost made love to him. Would have. But he'd gone, and it hadn't taken her long to figure out why.

Gram had filled his head with notions about her. The people in town had colored in the details. Brad had said all along he believed the real Carolina was passionate and wanting. She'd gone and proved him right.

"And that's all the man needed to know," she murmured into her glass.

All those years of telling herself she was different from the other women in her family, secretly fearing she was lacking because of it, unable to love. At the same time hoping that difference would be her strength, would save her from the pain and mistakes of loving too much. All those years down the drain.

In Brad's arms she became just another Palmette, careless and passionate and fearless. And painfully aware it showed.

The bell strip jangled on the door. He slid onto the seat across from her, suit crumpled and sun-soaked, hair combed back with a quick rake of his fingers.

A patron called out from a booth on the opposite wall. "What put the bounce in your step, Lavalier?"

Brad chuckled and shook his head. "Don't ask, Bill, don't ask."

Carolina glared at her silverware, a tinge of color in her cheeks, her voice soft but sharp. "Why don't you take out an ad?"

Brad's smile faded fast, reappearing for Charlene and the menus. "Thanks, sugar." He handed one to Carolina, speaking only when they were alone again. "Either you trust me enough to keep this private or you don't."

"This? Nothing's happened." Her look challenged him to say otherwise.

Brad sucked on an ice cube, grinding it between his teeth. He winced when it hit his sensitive back tooth. He saw through the anger easily enough; she was hurting. And he was at fault. "I'd say a lot happened. Our relationship came quite a way yesterday."

She wouldn't quibble about the word "relationship." "Not all the way."

"I want you to know that was my fault."

"Was it? I believe you proved a pet theory of yours. Who could blame you for testing it when the chance fell right into your—your lap like that. Smile, you were proved right."

The asphalt wasn't the only thing hot enough to fry eggs on. His glare was enough to singe holes in the back of her menu. He reached over and bent the plastic-coated paper she hid behind. "I was proved wrong."

He wouldn't provoke her into asking how.

"You're as ripe and passionate as I ever said you were, but you're not ready."

"The peach ripe for plucking? Or should that be—" She didn't finish the sentence.

"The fact is," he ground out, "I was willing to do anything to get you in bed. I wanted you, that's why I left."

"Complicated theory."

Not as complicated as the woman across from him, Brad thought. At least fantasies turned out the way you wanted them to. Real women were more difficult. And more fragile.

"I didn't leave because there was no more left to learn. We have a *long* way to go, darlin'. I want you with me every step of the way, eyes open, not blinded by stars."

She stared at the Formica in front of her, white embedded with twinkling gold. "So you left because you wanted to stay."

"You weren't ready."

"Shouldn't I decide that?"

"Ready to jump in bed maybe."

"Lower your voice, please."

It was already gratingly low. "Do you want everyone to know I was murmuring seductively to you in Giroux's?"

"Certainly not."

"Then I'm still right."

She scowled. It didn't fool him for a minute. That fierce pride was a shield. Knowing he'd left her for the best of reasons didn't help. "I was trying to spare you this," he said.

"What?"

"This." He glanced around the room. Her gaze followed, until she spotted too many people looking back.

"Wouldn't it be harder to face them if something had happened yesterday?" he asked. "You're blushing even now."

"It's ninety-seven degrees, I'm flushed." But in the long pause that followed, she had to admit he had a point. "Would it have hurt to talk it over with me first?"

He grinned, a playful leer. "It hurt plenty. I could barely walk back to my cottage."

She snorted daintily and took a long sip of water. "I was waiting," she said in that silky contralto, peering over the rim of her glass at him.

He cleared his throat loudly and snapped open the napkin on his lap. "I know you were."

A few moments passed as they studied each other, messages moving silently, doubts flickering like heat waves.

"Was I wrong?" he asked. "Giving you a way out?"

Yes. She wanted to say it so badly, it hurt. Her gaze dropped to the table. She wanted him, but she was afraid, afraid if he saw it, everyone would. They'd see how she longed for him, the way she trembled at his touch, floated like a cloud on the low murmur of his voice, how her heart soared just watching him cross the street. She would have loved him if he'd given her the chance.

She was deeply afraid she loved him now.

How could a woman hide that? How could a woman in love not give herself away? And the next thing you knew, she'd be the talk of the town. Again.

"I wanted to give us more time," Brad was saying, unconsciously slipping his pocket watch out, winding the stem until it stiffened. "Time for everyone to get used to seeing us together. A person can adjust to small towns, you know."

She nodded, wondering if that watch wasn't wound tight enough to run till Christmas.

"I didn't want you worrying what people think," he concluded.

People? The only public opinion she cared about seemed to have shrunk to one man. "I'm not always like that."

He knew. She caught fire for him and him alone. A queer sort of pride stirred in him. "I thought two things, maybe that's why my timing was so bad—it took me a minute to decide between them."

"And they were?"

"That you were everything I'd waited for in a woman. Passionate, eager, giving. And that I was capable of using your passion to get what I wanted out of the moment. That staggered me."

It had affected him that much? A hollow opened up in Carolina at his words, a hole no lunch would fill.

"Ready to order?" Charlene stopped at the edge of the table.

Carolina read off the first item that caught her eye. "Jambalaya."

"Make it two," Brad said.

"I'll leave you alone, then." Charlene winked and waltzed off.

Carolina sighed. "This whole town wants to play matchmaker."

"That's just their way."

"Think they'd lose interest if we stopped meeting? If you stopped calling me down to your office twice a week to discuss the case?"

Part of him went cold. He'd rushed her, and he was paying the consequences. All his lofty talk about stopping just in time didn't count for beans. She managed to sit calmly across the booth from him while running headlong in the opposite direction.

But he hadn't lost her yet. He tucked the watch in his pocket and covered her hand with his. "Ever think they might be right? That maybe we belong together?" He surreptitiously skimmed her palm with his thumb.

She pulled her hand into her lap and crinkled the

napkin lying there. "I don't know if I'm ready to plop back into the goldfish bowl."

"Never know unless you try."

Truer words were never spoken. When was she going to stop hiding and take the risk? And when would she ever meet a man like Brad Lavalier to take it with?

Brad leaned back so Charlene could set their plates down.

"Do you have mint tea?" Carolina asked.

"Like Eve's? You know we do." The waitress touched Carolina's arm. "And you know we miss her something fierce around here."

Carolina thanked her sincerely. It was touching the way people went out of their way to stop her and talk about Gram. They *were* concerned. They *did* care. They also said things like "It must be awful lonely out there in that house all by yourself."

Brad avoided her I-told-you-so glance. "Yes. But her things are there. It's as if she's still around."

"And smilin' down," Charlene said, patting Carolina's shoulder as she sashayed back to the counter. "Smilin' down, honey."

Carolina had to laugh. "See what I mean? Everybody sees through this arrangement."

"What arrangement?" he asked ingenuously.

"You can't be a lawyer and be that naive. Gram set us up, and you know it."

He chuckled. "I knew it the day she came to me with that addendum to her will."

"And you did nothing about it?"

He shrugged. "She was always trying to get us to meet."

Underneath that lackadaisical demeanor was a man, a firebrand—long and lean and ready to mark her his.

Carolina dug into the steaming plate of rice. They went heavy on the spice at Giroux's. It was like adding gasoline to a volcano, like steam heat mixed with thoughts of Brad Lavalier kissing her in the rain.

He slid the Tabasco to her side of the table, his hand nudging hers. His ankle whispered against the silk of her hose, making her keenly aware of the skin they encased.

"Counselor?" she stated coolly, as much for the passing waitress's benefit as his.

"Yes, ma'am?"

Her consonants were as clipped and cool as her subtly northern accent. "I may have consented to meet you in public, but I did not consent to playing footsie."

He grinned and sprinkled some Tabasco on her jambalaya. "Live dangerously."

Slowly, deliberately, he took her hand, turning it palm up. He placed an ice cube there, covering her hand with his, fingers laced. In seconds her palm went numb—the rest of her became meltingly hot.

"What do people see?" he asked softly. "Two joined hands. That's all. Does anyone really know what goes on between a man and a woman alone?"

Minutes inched by. Water trickled out between their fingers. The ice disappeared, his palm pressed hers. Skin on skin produced contact, contact friction, and friction liquid.

Eventually he let go, blotting the table with a napkin.

He winked. "Don't worry, the wet spot's mine."

The waitress placed an iced tea in front of Carolina. "Here you go, honey. Looks like you could use a little cooling off."

Eight

She could use a hole in her head to vent the steam.

"Brad."

"Yes, darlin'?" He waited, innocent and wide-eyed, for her comment.

"Don't do that again."

"Cross my heart."

Carolina figured she'd have *her* heart examined—as soon as the experts finished with her brain. Brad was bound and determined that the clientele of Giroux's would bear witness to their budding courtship. Fine. Right now she didn't care. They saw nothing but the surface. Only the man across from her knew how close they'd come to consummating this relationship. And he was pleasantly busy undressing her with his eyes.

She wore a soft white dress that draped from her shoulders; she was learning to dress for the heat. Maybe it was his heat. The temperature rose a good ten degrees when he was around.

A belt of braided gold rope cinched her waist. The clothes she'd worn the previous day had been too loose, too easy. A person needed a picklock to unbuckle this belt. Her hair, slick and straight in the rain, was tightly braided this time. A floppy bow of salmon pink dangled between her shoulder blades, doing what it could to camouflage the tension coiling there.

"You want me to be more discreet," he stated.

She wanted not to catch fire every time she saw him.

She wanted to run away, back up North where no one knew her the way they did here. And she wanted very much not to hurt him when she did.

It had to be kinder to let him go before this got any worse. To stop leading them both on. On all her previous returns to Grelickville, her security rested on her self-contained public persona. That control was slipping. She was hanging by her fingernails on a cliff face. Someone had to shout a warning.

"I'm not in love with you," she said flatly.

Brad's fork hit the Formica and pinged end over end to the floor.

"Gotcha a slippery one there, counselor." The waitress bustled over, replacing it with one from her apron pocket. "Yell if you need anything."

"Thanks." Brad turned back to Carolina. "Should I thank you for the warning too?"

His blunt tone didn't hide the pain. She'd hoped saying it would make it true. Would make him back off. She didn't want to hurt him—she wanted to protect them both from a passion on the verge of overspilling. "Things got out of hand, that's all."

"Your hands or mine?" he retorted, voice dangerously low.

"You wanted to talk, this is it. I don't want to love you."

He paused for a fraction of a second while tearing off a crust of bread. It didn't take a lawyer to figure out there was quite a difference between not loving and not wanting to love.

Lavalier, you've known it all the time. He could fire her passions more easily than banish her fears. And the fear hurt—seeing the longing she wanted to hide from him and couldn't. The woman needed love and didn't know how to ask.

But there was more to love than bodies. Wooing her properly, the way she thought she needed, would take time, time they didn't have. "You want to hear what I've learned about Shepherd?"

"Yes." Carolina exhaled and consciously relaxed her shoulders. She should celebrate this victory of common sense over hormones. But this aching emptiness wasn't hunger. Forcing down another spoonful of jambalaya wouldn't solve it. "Last time we talked you were going to check out his past."

Wrong, Carolina's conscience chided. The last time they'd talked, Brad had been calling her sugar, peaches, cream. Anything juicy and sweet. Shepherd had had nothing to do with it.

But Brad played along. "I hired a private detective."

"What did he find out?"

"He hasn't started working yet."

"Why not?"

"Because I needed your permission to pay him. You didn't give me carte blanche on the retainer."

"You know I'll do anything to save the house."

"Anything?" He crooked a brow and grinned.

She scowled.

"Good," he said, as if that were an answer. Smacking his lips, he added another dash of Tabasco. "I was hoping you weren't kissing me just to get this settled."

"You know that isn't the reason."

"Then what is? We've ruled out love."

She tapped her long nails on the table. "Back to the reverend, please?"

"We've been going slow."

"So I noticed."

"You want me to move faster?"

"They way you move is just fine," she snapped.

Mrs. Feydeau smiled sweetly as she made her way

to the cashier, her ninety-five-year-old mother in tow. "Afternoon, Carolina. Brad."

Carolina glared across the table at her companion.

"Don't look at me," he replied blandly, "I didn't announce it. And Carolina?"

"What."

"I'm glad you like the way I move." He winked.

She crushed another napkin in her hand.

He pinned her eyes with his, the joking over with. That look said it all. He wanted her. He planned to have her. When she was ready. And when they were alone.

But there was only so much a man could say with a look. He spelled out the rest, his voice throaty and low. "You can't resist me when I touch you. Do you have any idea how that makes a man feel?"

From the flush on her cheeks, he knew how it made her feel.

"Please don't tell me here."

He cleared his throat and let the tabasco clear his sinuses. He'd made his point. "I figured if we moved too fast, we might scare Shepherd off altogether. I want him to know we're keeping an eye on him, that's all."

"But wouldn't his leaving town get Gram's land back?"

"What about my other clients? Some of them have invested with him too."

"As I told Dotty yesterday, investing and donating are two different things."

"Thank you, Miss Financial Consultant." The teasing tone didn't take.

Carolina smiled grimly. "Sorry. It's just frustrating."

"I'm as frustrated as you, darlin'."

The waitress popped up again. "Everything all right here? Besides the frustration, I mean?"

Carolina clenched her teeth. "Wonderful."

"Mr. Lavalier, you have a call."

Brad nodded to Charlene, studying Carolina when they were alone again. "And we've got a lot more talking to do."

"About the reverend? Pay the private detective."

Brad frowned and stood up. "About us." He leaned over her, one hand clenching the back of the booth, the other a loose fist knuckle-down on the tabletop. "I'm not saying another word about Shepherd until we've settled what's between us first."

"Is that an ultimatum?"

It was a gamble, plain as day to a lawyer throwing himself on the mercy of the court. He caught her chin between his thumb and forefinger, and, with the whole restaurant watching, kissed her long and slow. "No matter what else we might end up doing, sugar, we'll talk first."

He strode to the phone booth, his cocky grin reflected in the folding doors. Let 'em all look, he thought. This whole town could know how he felt. He wasn't hiding *his* light under a bushel. However, he did have to squeeze it into a phone booth first.

"Lavalier here." He bumped his knees on the metal seat and cursed. These places weren't designed with six-foot three-inch men in mind.

"Mr. Lavalier, you've gotta come down to the jail. I been here all night and they—"

Joe Perkins. Town drunk.

The routine was, well, routine. Brad would arrange bail and an escort to accompany Joe to the AA meeting at the town hall basement. Otherwise the man would wander over to the Chevalier Bar and it would start all over. "Why'd they pick you up, Joe?"

"General principles, counselor, general principles. A man can't get a good night's sleep around here."

No, a man couldn't, Brad thought. He'd barely slept at all, caught between hot sheets and hotter memories.

He maneuvered the doors shut so the overhead fan would turn on. He'd felt prickly since the day before, his skin as raw and oversensitive as his conscience. The sheets hadn't let him sleep. The muggy air taunted him, lying on him in an empty bed. That morning his showerhead spurted and pummeled him, beating on his skin, replacing sweat with dampness. Shaving was an invitation to relive her touch, the skin of her palm over his cheek, the look of wonder in her eyes.

He could have sworn he'd seen love. Or was that merely a reflection of his own emotions? A projection of his hopes? A sop to his conscience? He shouldn't have walked out on her. He should have stayed and talked this out.

Listening to Joe Perkins rant about jailhouse conditions, Brad reached his conclusion. He owed Carolina some conversation. About love. About doubts. About taking time. He'd tell her he loved her before their bodies said it for them.

And if she didn't buy it, he'd rent a billboard and let the whole town tell her.

Furiously scanning the room, Carolina watched the few remaining patrons take a sudden intense interest in their plates.

Her lips still tingled. *You'd think you'd been kissed by Elvis*, she thought, frowning as she dabbed them with a napkin. What was she going to do with the man? She'd told him she didn't love him. It had gone right over his head.

Deny it all you want, a small voice inside her said. A woman couldn't yield to a man on a wicker settee and then pretend nothing had happened.

If only I hadn't given him that darn umbrella. A pesky detail. As if altering that action could have prevented every breathtaking touch that followed, every pleading kiss. No matter how many times she relived it, the movie played back the same.

"In 3-D *and* Sensurround," she said with a moan.

What had happened between them couldn't be blamed on lust or heat or a sudden change in the weather. On inhibitions falling like rain. What had happened was the result of love, his tenderness, his humor, his unspoken challenges, his daring her to be the woman she'd always glimpsed from afar. He'd seen that woman—revealed in private moments only. And at the last moment, he'd refused to take advantage of her crumbling defenses.

She wasn't sure she loved him for that or not. She only knew she was beginning to love him no matter what.

One step at a time, she thought, mentally adding up the bill before counting out her change. Brad would object to her buying, but Brad wasn't there. She had things to do, people to see.

It all went back to Gram. She'd set this whole thing up, probably from the moment she'd begun referring to the house as Carolina's trousseau. As every romantic southern woman knew, a woman made her own trousseau. So it was up to Carolina to save that house.

She marched out the door, head high, shoulders back. The racket of Brad Lavalier rapidly extricating himself from that glass matchbox clattered behind her. The jangling bells limply said her good-bye.

Carolina parked her car on the flattened-grass parking lot. The diagonal of a frayed tent rope pointed the way to the house trailer that served as Reverend Shepherd's portable headquarters.

She felt confident, prepared. She might even be in love. But that would have to wait until the rest of this was settled. After all, if she didn't get the land, she'd lose the house. Without the house there'd be no reason to stay in Grelickville. If she left Grelickville, she'd be leaving Brad.

They hadn't made any promises, of that she was

very aware. But the field had to be cleared first. Literally.

Before she could knock, two of Shepherd's burly assistants lumbered out the door. Carolina squeezed against the rail to let them pass.

The reverend paused in the doorway, grinning as if down from on high. "Why Mizz Palmette, mighty pleased you stopped by."

"Reverend. I believe we have a few matters to discuss." She should have done this from the start, she thought, striding into the darkly paneled interior and waiting for her eyes to adjust.

The entire trailer vibrated with the air conditioner's effort.

"Have yourself a seat, young lady."

Carolina eyed the grainy plastic that passed for leather chair-covers. She could imagine peeling herself off of one when this interview was finished. Nervous perspiration had started already.

"I've been meanin' to call," the reverend intoned, wiping the smile off his face with a handkerchief, replacing it with an expression of appropriate sincerity. "I wanted to offer my personal condolences on your lovely grandmother's recent passing."

"Thank you."

"She'll be missed."

"She already is."

Carolina watched the flame from Shepherd's lighter bounce higher with each puff as he lit a cigar. Only the foolhardy went looking for more heat in this weather, she thought, then remembered her dish of jambalya sprinkled with Tabasco, and Brad's parting kiss. She'd have to talk to him about that. "Reverend, I have a proposition I believe you'd be interested in hearing."

Shepherd strolled behind a mahogany desk that must have been in someone else's family for generations. Glancing at the door, Carolina wondered how they'd shoehorned it in. Silly question. She knew the truly greedy would do just about anything to accumulate more—she hadn't worked in finance for six years without learning that.

The reverend interrupted her as she sized up the rest of the furnishings. "Where's your lawyer friend?"

"He's not exactly a friend," she replied, consciously slowing down her words. Denials, especially swift ones, often gave rise to more speculation. A comfortable southern drawl would make her sound more at ease. She used it. "Ah'm here on my own."

Shepherd jerked down the curling corner of his vest, drew his suit jacket over his spreading middle, and settled himself in a huge swivel chair on the other side of the desk. "To what purpose?"

"I want the land," she replied.

What else? he seemed to say, his bushy brows rising in tandem. He slicked back the silvery waves in his hair, pinkie ring glinting. "I was deeply honored by your grandmother's bequest. She was a devout and generous woman."

"And for some reason, she chose you to have the house if I left town."

"Someone has to take care of the property."

"I'd never let it fall into disrepair."

He nodded slowly, the big chair bouncing softly. Brad had a habit of doing the same. Carolina forcibly removed him from her mind.

"What do you suppose your grandmother's motives were in making this unusual arrangement?"

"I'm sure she intended giving you time to find another setting for your meetings."

He chuckled unpleasantly. "Try another one."

Carolina crossed her legs. "Love, then."

"I wasn't romancing your grandmother."

"No, but I believe she got it in her head *I* could find love here."

"Have you?"

"I'd appreciate it if we could return to the subject."

"Which are your grandmother's wishes. Which I

intend to abide by." He waved the cigar her way, interrupting the stream of smoke rising toward the ceiling. "Maybe it's this lawyer fella who's stirring up doubts."

More than one, Carolina thought wryly.

"Maybe he's looking to tie you up in some long legal affair."

That wasn't the kind of affair she was afraid of. "Divide and conquer, Reverend? I'm afraid it won't work. I trust Mr. Lavalier's advice. However, I believe we can settle this privately. I'm offering to buy back that land." It was an expensive way to go, but as a last resort, she'd use it.

Shepherd leaned back in his chair, watching a halo of smoke drift over his head. "It isn't exactly mine to sell."

"I realize that. Which is why I propose paying you the value of it in return for your leaving. That way it reverts to me in accordance with the will."

Shepherd smiled, this time genuinely. "The people here have been very good to me."

"When you've milked them dry, you'll move on."

"You have a negative attitude toward religion."

She rose slowly. "I call what you do fund-raising, when I'm in a generous mood."

Shepherd absently picked at the leaf wrapping of his cigar with a manicured thumbnail. "Speakin' of funds. How do you intend running that big old house on one salary? Or is that young lawyer gonna help you out?"

Carolina squared her shoulders. That was easy to deny. "He's never given me a penny." Unlike the two she'd given Shepherd. She allowed herself a thin smile as she turned to leave. She'd give him a few days to think over the offer.

The reverend didn't bother to rise. His words carried across the cramped room. "I understand this fella's doing a lot of helping out around your place.

Dropping by in the afternoon. Offering rides. Maybe doin' a little work on that back porch?"

The air-conditioning had nothing to do with the chill that coursed through Carolina's blood. The sick feeling wasn't from the lunch she'd barely touched, it was from the smile on Shepherd's face, the confidence with which he laid out his insinuations like playing cards on the surface of that mahogany desk, like palmed aces.

Defenses tumbled through her mind. That back porch had needed work for years; Gram talked about it often.

That didn't stop her remembering Brad leading her up those stairs, one creaking step at a time.

The railing swaying against their weight.

The roof leaking, dripping cold water on her bared shoulders while his mouth . . .

"As I understand it," she said, voice papery and dry, "Mr. Lavalier helped Gram with many projects around the house. I don't need such assistance."

"And what, pray tell, does a beautiful woman like you need?"

To get out of there. To breathe clean air. Muggy and suffocating as the heat might be, it was better than standing there trembling. She fervently hoped he wouldn't see her hand shake on the doorknob.

"Good day, Reverend."

Think about my offer.
Call me when you're ready to sell.
My lawyer will be in touch.
She knew all those perfectly respectable closing lines, and she hadn't had the presence of mind to use any of them. Especially the last. She'd been lucky to get out of there without tripping over her own feet.

Hours later, her stomach lurched when she recalled the smile on Shepherd's face, the assurance of his accusation, the weakness of her rejoinder.

"Gram needed help around the house! Oh Lordy. I need a plane ticket to Boston," she said with a groan.

What she needed was Brad. She had to talk to him. He was the only one she could turn to.

All right, so she was spooked, crumbling before the specter of scandal. The only way Brad could save her from it would be by staying away. The very idea hurt. He'd become part of her life, insinuating himself into her memories, her house, the way the heat touched her all over.

But if the most private part of this affair was in danger of becoming public, they'd have to stay apart.

The night was calmly working its way to a swelter. Brad's imagination, firing like a furnace, paled beside the temperature of his skin. He strode into the small cottage kitchen, determined to get his mind off Carolina.

Running four hard miles hadn't worked. A quick shower hadn't either. Even DeVoe's dog, chasing him half a mile up the Quantico Road, couldn't take his mind off the heat.

"Ought to get a writ for the mangy animal."

But that wasn't causing his irritation, and he knew it. Restlessly he stood in front of his refrigerator, stripped to the waist, wearing nothing but a hastily donned pair of dry running shorts.

He was frustrated, pure and simple. He was making every move he knew how to win the woman, but she had to have her say in this. Between her wanting eyes, her giving mouth, and her firm denials of love, he was feeling thoroughly tossed and bossed.

"Which is it, Carolina? You love me or you don't."

The only decision he felt free to make on his own was between a beer, a cooler, or a straight shot of sipping whiskey.

He settled for a peach cooler. Normally he despised

the things, but he'd bought the six-pack in case she stopped by to talk.

Fool.

Twisting off the cap, the aluminum foil crinkled in his hand, and he wondered for the hundredth time what he'd say, what she'd say, how he could get her to stay.

He'd apologized for leaving her high and not so dry the day before, hadn't he? Apologized for thinking with his belt buckle. For leaving both of them jumpy and raw.

He wanted to love her. To tell her and show her. He wanted to be a man about it, not a lovesick boy. He wanted to take control. That public kiss was one way; the next move was hers.

He reached the phone on the first ring. Didn't answer it until the second. It took him that long to down the last of the cooler and dredge up his courage. It wasn't every day you told a woman you loved her.

"He hasn't called!"

Brad immediately recognized the querulous voice of his eighty-six-year-old client. "Mrs. Boudrine."

"They been married three months today. I remember. I send flowers. But do they call with a simple thank-you?"

"I'm sure it was overlooked."

"I will not be overlooked, young man! I'm grand-mother to that ungrateful young'un and great-grand-mother to whatever they've got on the way. Married three months, and she's five months pregnant if she's a day. You think I don't know what goes on in this town? I don't miss a lick. I tell you I'm changing my will."

For the fourth time in two years, Brad calculated. "Would you like to come on down to the office some time next week?" That'd give her time to cool down. He wiped the empty bottle across his forehead and let her talk him into an appointment for the next day.

After another ten minutes of "uh-huh's" and "yes-sum's" he managed to get off the phone. No closer to answers than when he'd picked it up.

The knock on the door set his heart pumping harder than his four mile run had. "Lavalier, you got it bad," he said aloud.

He swung the door open. Night sounds ricocheted off the trees. The smell of night blossoms hit him, lush and thick and sweet. Carolina stepped from the dark into the pool of yellow porch light. She looked like a lost goddess, hazel eyes wavering and uncertain. Her flimsy cotton dress caught a breeze.

Brad swallowed hard and grinned for all he was worth. He would put her at ease if it killed him. "I thought you'd never get here, sugar."

"Stuff it, Lavalier."

She marched past him, shoulders squared enough to balance I-beams on. Apparently she needed that much moxie to make an appearance at his door. Too bad she'd summoned it a second after he glimpsed the doubts.

"We have to talk," she announced.

"Have a seat." His professional tone soothed her a bit, but she declined.

"I don't believe we should see each other again. The reverend suspects."

"Last I heard, so does half the town."

She glared at him. "Whose fault is that? Sometimes I wonder whose side you're really on."

He grinned and sidled by her, heading into the kitchen with his empty. "I like the left side. Although I'll sleep on the right if you prefer."

It had taken her until five to stop shaking, until eight to pick up the phone, and all of five minutes to get down there when she got a busy signal. She was going to put a stop to this once and for all. "We are not having an affair."

He flashed her a dubious look. "We already are, in everything but actual fact."

She threw up her hands. "Only a lawyer would come up with that split hair."

"Why, 'Lina, I've never seen you so riled."

"I don't want this whole town talking."

"Don't you love me?"

"Don't change the subject."

"I thought that was the subject," he replied lightly. He tossed his bottle into a trash canister and opened the refrigerator again. "What are you drinking?"

"A double of anything." She squinted at the fluorescent ring of light. "This room hasn't changed since Henry's day."

"Now who's changing the subject?" His fingers touched hers as he handed her a cooler. "Thought this might go down easier than whiskey. We have a long night ahead of us."

Nine

Carolina got control of herself. "First we talk about Shepherd."

"And since Shepherd knows, that brings us back to us." He sauntered past her into the living room.

"Uh-uh. Shepherd *suspects*. In which case, I don't think we should see each other. For a while," she amended.

Brad spread his arms wide and swung around to face her. "You're seeing me now, sugar." He wore nothing but gray jogging shorts and a grin. Everything else was as bare as nature intended when a man and woman were alone at night.

"Why did I ever think I could simply talk to you?" Carolina muttered in exasperation, looking everywhere but at him. She wound her hand around the neck of the bottle until she'd almost strangled it. "I'm here to talk about Shepherd; you can stop showing off."

"Ah do declare, Ah detect a compliment there."

"Drop it. We've got to organize our opposition."

"You're always organized, 'Lina." He took the bottle back, efficiently twisting off the cap. "Every *i* dotted, every *t* crossed."

"I'm talking about cleaning up loose ends. I need to

know if the house is mine or not, before anything else."

"You want everything neat and clean."

"Yes." Clean, as in the smell of soap, the lingering dampness of a shower. She'd seen him come back from his run drenched and haggard. Now he practically sparkled. Up close his body was sleek muscle, a sheen of taut skin. The man probably never gained an ounce. A surge of perfectly unreasonable resentment buoyed her flagging resolve immensely, and she gulped the wine cooler. "I'm in no mood to banter, Brad. I intended toppling Shepherd from the start."

"And toppled me instead."

"I explained that mistake at lunch."

"Felt all right to me." He padded back into the kitchen, for some reason too charged to sit down.

"That was before I saw Shepherd."

"You *saw* him?" Leaning back from the open fridge, abdomen rippling, nipples tightened by the cold, he took a sudden interest in the conversation.

Carolina took a sudden interest in the carpet.

"You run into him downtown?"

"I went to his office," she said, battling a twinge of guilt.

"A lawyer can come in handy for those things, 'Lina. Why didn't you tell me?"

"I thought it was up to me to settle it."

In the kitchen, ice cubes broke free of their tin with a screech of cold metal. Finally Brad spoke. "I'm here to help you. I never said I wouldn't."

"Only that you were in no hurry."

"And you are?"

"I want to see some progress made."

Funny, he was watching the progress they'd made slip away. "He doesn't want to settle," Brad said, carrying a beer into the living room. "I checked that out first."

"Apparently my lawyer doesn't want to settle either."

"No?" He got a lot of caution into one word.

"I believe he wants me to stay in Grelickville."

"If that means me, I suppose he does." Brad took a seat across from the coffee table, a squeaky rattan chair with a swivel base. He swung it slowly back and forth, one ankle resting on his knee. His voice was very soft. "Are you that worried about talk?"

"Shepherd said you'd be a good one to help me out on the back porch."

His chair rocked to a halt. "A guess. But."

"But."

"I don't brag in locker rooms, sugar." The words were more reassuring than the chilly way he said them.

"I didn't say you did. But how else would he know? There's no way he could have seen us."

Brad shrugged. Carolina tried not to stare at the expanse of bare chest. Or the guardedness in his eyes. "I'm sorry, I'm just saying he's suspicious and it hit very close to home."

"I can see it did," he replied.

"I've fought this reputation all my life, that I'd turn out like Gram or Mom. I *won't* be talked about."

"You will be if you live here. Or else you'll never love anyone at all." It was softly inflected, like a question. "Do you love anyone, 'Lina?"

She wouldn't meet his gaze. "There can't be an 'us' if it's going to be all over town. That may be unreasonable, but those are my terms."

"And if we can't prove anything against the man, and he stays around?"

Carolina drained her cooler, gripping it tightly. "I offered to buy the land."

Brad winced. "How?"

"With a loan. The equity on the house would be collateral."

"And how do you expect to pay it off with two houses to keep up?"

"I'd have to sell the condo. It's possible I could work

down here, especially if I drum up more business in the area." She took in his silence, his frown. "You don't like the idea."

"Maybe I'm vain enough to want you coming down here because of me. Not because I let Eve give her land away and couldn't get it back."

Carolina sighed. "I don't mean it that way."

The corner of his mouth crooked. "Maybe that's just the way people'll see it."

"The hell with what people think."

"Bravo," he muttered. "So I live here, you live at the house, and we don't see each other until Shepherd leaves town. How's this gonna work, 'Lina?"

"I don't know," she replied miserably. She'd offered to move to Grelickville—he clearly wasn't thrilled at the prospect. Part of her had secretly hoped . . . "Maybe it's time to realize Gram filled both our heads with a lot of romantic nonsense that'll never come true."

Brad shook his head, jaw clenched. "It's true. I've seen it, touched it, tasted it." He got up, stood next to her, ran a hand down her arm, aware of what few clothes he had on and the way they fit his body. Aware of hers, inside that filmy opaque layer of white cloth. "We were both ready as two lit sticks of dynamite yesterday, and no amount of water in the world could quench that."

"I'm quenching it now."

"Good." He picked up her empty bottle. "Then I'll fetch you another so you can make sure it's out."

She trailed after him into the kitchen. "You know what I mean."

"And what you feel like. And how you look when I've got my hands on you. I left before we could talk yesterday. I had some things I should have said."

She had an idea what was coming. She didn't want to hear it, not spoken over the undercurrent of impatience and anger she sensed in him. "Brad."

He worked his jaw a minute, letting the open

refrigerator cool him off. Finally he spoke. "Would saying 'I love you' make any difference?"

"Brad."

"You heard me."

"Call it anything else," she pleaded. "Lust, heat lightning, sheet lightning. Not love."

"I didn't say you had to return the feelin'. I just thought you should know."

Her heart cracked. For all his infuriating persistence, how could the man walk away from a declaration like that?

"Aren't you going to fight?" she asked.

"Nothin' else to say."

She retreated to the living room, feeling bereft but not sure why, feeling miles away from him, although the cottage was very small.

She sagged on the sofa, wiping strands of hair plastered against her neck. She glanced at stacks of haphazardly shelved books, at the stylish but well-used furniture that spelled bachelorhood. She peeked in the bedroom and wondered if that pile of books on the end table meant he'd been having as much trouble sleeping as she.

But all her pacing couldn't take her away from the words he'd spoken. He loved her. And she didn't have the courage to say the same.

"Ever hear of prenuptial agreements?" she called.

"I've heard of them," he said from the kitchen, packing ice in a glass.

"I meant mine."

There was no sound from the other room this time. Carolina took a steadying breath. It was easier saying this without worrying about the look on his face, the scorn. She watched his reflection in a mirror; he stood at the sink, looking out at the night for a long time.

"I got engaged to a boy from Opelousas. It wasn't what Gram had always promised, not in the way of romance or fireworks or moonlight. But he was decent, kind. And I—"

"You what?" Brad stood in the kitchen doorway. Her gentle suitor was gone, a guarded, tension-stilled man in his place. "You what, Carolina?"

She shrugged, shamefaced. "I was afraid of the kind of love Gram talked about, the kind I saw overwhelming people, changing their lives forever. He was safe."

"So why didn't you marry him?"

"I wanted it in writing first. I insisted on a prenuptial agreement, stating that I'd complete college, that the house would be mine in case of a divorce. It even specified how many days a year we could be apart." The sigh shook her but she met his gaze this time. "Aren't you going to laugh?"

"I don't think it's funny."

"People in town did. When word got around. I was the laughingstock of Grelickville. 'Imagine,' they said, 'trying to legislate love. Ain't that just like a Palmette.'"

Brad grunted.

"Well, it wasn't," Carolina declared. "It's about as far from a Palmette as you can get. Gram was mortified when she found out. Said 'If you have to write it down, it's no more real than the paper it's printed on. Love is heart's blood, not ink.'"

Only when Carolina closed her eyes tight did the tears break free. That's when she realized she'd been choking them back all along. "I'm surprised you haven't heard the story."

"I have. Some of it."

Her stunned look soon faltered, and she glanced away.

Brad went into the bathroom and came out with a tissue and a damp washcloth. "Here."

His voice was gruff, but not from anger. "People make mistakes, you know, especially where love's concerned."

"And Palmettes make them in big, splashy ways. People asked me why I didn't just take out an ad with all my specifications spelled out up front."

"That was a while back."

"Six years."

"So who is it you're not forgiving? Them for laughing or you for being human?"

"Human meaning scared? But I still am. What if I'm what Gram always said I was, a true Palmette underneath it all? You wouldn't want me throwing my whole life over and living for you alone."

Wouldn't he? He'd scale mountains for that privilege, fight dragons. And face down any townful of people if it meant keeping her from crying again, anguished and alone.

It might seem selfish, but a man who was ready to turn his own world upside down for total, life-changing, necessary love wanted no less in return.

"You want to know a secret or two about me?" he asked.

She sniffed. "What?"

"The reason I left my job. I'm still not sure I wasn't played for a chump. Ever hear of Pearl River Estates?"

"No."

"It was a development I helped put through, not without a lot of opposition. It required some fancy legal footwork and an end run around a town zoning commission."

"That's just big business, isn't it?"

"So they say. But the plans for this project included tearing down a senior citizens' complex on the proposed site. It was old, run-down, but home for a lot of people who couldn't adapt very well to finding lodgings elsewhere. That's what winning meant; disrupting people's lives so my employers could make millions."

"I can't picture you doing that."

"Didn't know I was, at first. They played me per-

fectly, convincing me so I could convince the zoning
people that there'd be places set aside in the new
project for the seniors. How it would improve their
standard of living and all that. When construction
started, plans changed, and those forty housing
units never did materialize. By then it was too late for
the people who'd been displaced. I walked out, came
up here to Uncle Julius's office. Looking for something." He peered at her, hoping she'd understand.
Hoping she wouldn't see him as harshly as he saw
himself sometimes. Hoping she'd give him a chance
to come to her rescue, and get it right this time.

"Did you find what you were looking for?" she
asked quietly.

"After three years I was beginning to think I had
nothing to show for it except a hand-me-down office,
a rented cottage, and a leased car. Not my idea of a
successful life." He studied the table a long time. "Eve
suggested another one. It has to do with family. A
wife. I might be in no hurry to get what I want,
Carolina, but I'm not fool enough to let it slip through
my fingers when I find it."

He ran a hand through the hair that trailed over
her shoulders, fanning over the back of the sofa.

The phone rang. He cursed softly and picked it up.
After five minutes with a reconsidering Mrs. Boudrine, he hung up. "Sorry. Goes with the territory."

Carolina had been listening, not to the words, but
the tone of voice. He was patient, not patronizing.
She liked to think he'd paid Gram as much respect,
was as unhesitatingly kind. Some people would sell a
man like that short. Blame him for leaving his
practice in New Orleans. Some people would talk, but
then they always did.

"It was very brave, what you did," she said.

"A day late and a dollar short for the people involved." He sat back, exhaling a long breath, draping
an arm around shoulders bared by her summer
dress.

At first her skin tingled at the contact, then she nestled against his chest, his breath skimming her hair. "You're a good lawyer."

"I like helping people. Around here they come to me for more than loopholes. I know *why* Mrs. Boudrine is cutting her grandson out of her will, and why she'll put him back in a few months. I know when the DeVoe brothers are going to be taking another of their trips out of state—"

"Are they still running that moonshine operation?"

"Yep." He tucked her head back against his shoulder.

Carolina shook her head, her cheek rubbing him, a fond smile on her face. "The whole parish knows they do it."

"'Anything goes.'"

"'And nobody minds as long as everybody knows,'" they completed in unison. Brad had the rare pleasure of hearing her throaty laugh.

"Do the DeVoes avail themselves of your services, counselor?"

"Naturally. Every election year when the sheriff comes down on 'em. Although they've been known to pay in kind."

"Meaning?"

"I get a case of moonshine every Christmas."

Carolina gasped, scandalized and delighted. "And you're serving me store-bought?"

He chuckled. "I didn't think you'd appreciate pure 'shine."

"I'll tell you another secret. Gram used it too."

"Eve?" It was Brad's turn to be shocked.

"For colds. Vapor rub had nothing on DeVoe liquor."

She patted her chest, drawing Brad's eyes instantly down. It wasn't hundred-proof liquor building that fire in his belly. He almost swallowed the ice cube he'd been working on.

"This place is one long soap opera," Carolina

sighed. "And you fit right in." She nestled closer. "I think it's because you're a good listener."

He warmed at the compliment. "It helps to know what's going on."

"Purely professional interest, I'm sure."

"I've been known to put a tale or two on the grapevine myself. See how far it travels."

"That's cheating!"

"That's running it instead of it running you."

Carolina sensed a mild rebuke, but was too relaxed to chase it down. "If you like small towns, why live out here?"

"Same reason as you, privacy."

"Keep up with the news but not in it." She glanced at the phone. "You get no privacy from that."

"I turned it off this time."

It got quiet in the cottage, their link with the outside world severed at the push of a button.

"Someone might be trying to reach you," she said.

And he might be trying to reach her. "I'm officially off duty. Which means I can get you a shot of that Christmas 'shine." He winked and took off for the kitchen, returning with a shot glass, an unlabeled bottle of clear liquid, and a plan.

It began with sitting beside her on the sofa. "I'll be a gentleman and drink first."

"That's gentlemanly?"

"For a personal taste-tester it is." He threw his head back, downing the shot in one gulp. "To Grelickville," he sputtered when he could speak again.

"How's it taste?"

"Like the red stuff that leaks out of your radiator. Here."

She eyed it cautiously as she lifted the refilled glass to her lips. "To managing rumors."

A sip wouldn't do. Grimacing in advance, she threw it straight back. The fire behind her eyes receded as she wiped away the tears, gradually aware that the thumping in her lungs was Brad briskly patting her back.

"It wasn't a contest, 'Lina."

"Only way to get it down."

"Settles the nerves, as my own grandmother used to say."

She *had* been nervous, though for the life of her she couldn't remember why. "Turn that phone back on, Lavalier. You got clients in need."

He was looking at one. His lips touched hers, the smell of fire-eating liquor curiously sweet on her breath.

"Brad."

"We're going to get around to it eventually, sugar, why not now?"

"We were having such a nice conversation."

"It could get nicer."

She couldn't have agreed more, especially when he slipped his arm around her, running his fingers back into her hair.

Everything sharpened when she was around him, scents penetrated, air clung. She watched a moth battering a light bulb, thinking how the insect was fated to lose, destined to try. "I shouldn't have had those drinks."

"I'm not getting you drunk."

Oh yes he was. With those kisses, the sensation of breath on her ear. His voice vibrated so deep inside her, it seemed to meet up with her subconscious somewhere.

Crickets and darkness replaced rain and haze, bullfrogs and moss changed places with thunder and sweet wet grass. The man she'd run from, the town she'd feared, were welcoming her home, opening their arms.

She wanted to come home, to love someone the way Gram had always said it would happen. The way she'd feared. The way she'd dreamed. She wanted a man who knew her so well, she didn't have to ask him to kiss her just there. And heaven help her, she'd found him. "I should go."

He didn't dignify her statement with a response.

Her arm was bare, trapped between his chest and hers. The fabric of her dress was damp between them, thigh to thigh. She lifted her hand, but he laid his over it, pressing it softly down. "Touch me, sugar."

She made a muffled sound. Love didn't have to mean being swept away. Passion could be corralled. Alcohol didn't always dim the senses and free the inhibitions. Brad Lavalier did that just fine all by himself.

"I need to get back," she managed to say. Back to that empty house. *A man can fill up the empty spaces*, Gram seemed to whisper.

But Brad wasn't arguing. He knew full well he had to kiss her good-bye first, then walk her home, then kiss her again. This spiral of need wasn't stopping on the back porch. This time the screen door wouldn't slap shut between them. This time she'd welcome him in and he'd have the sense to follow.

The day before they'd reacted to need, desire. Now the emotions were mixed up with love. Foreordained, fated or cursed, it didn't matter. As long as she was sure. And there was only one place to convince her, to make the kinds of promises that would hold up in the light of day.

Somebody was righter than they knew when they called it going all the way.

"Take me home," she pleaded.

"Anything you say, sugar."

He tucked a kiss under her chin, his tongue-tip skimming her neck, raising goose bumps on over-heated flesh.

Her hand lifted to the dark rasp of beard at his throat.

His voice was equally rough, his legs shaky, when he picked the way along the path to the house, Carolina in his arms.

The night air slid by, fragrant and dense. The house loomed. A single bulb burned in the main hall to guide them from the kitchen.

"I've wanted to carry you up that staircase since the first time I saw you standing on it," he said, setting her on her feet. "Of course, you had a broomstick in your hand at the time."

"I believe we're a bit tangled to manage the stairs."

Tangled was right, legs and arms and mouths. His hand twisted in her hair. He could have sworn she'd worn it up tight when she'd entered his cottage.

Not now. One more kiss, searing, questing, less than tender, and he'd be sure it wasn't the moonshine making her so hot. He lifted his mouth from hers, holding her face between his hands, until he'd convinced himself it was love shining in those eyes.

"Think we can cool off long enough to walk that far?" He nodded toward the carved mahogany staircase overhanging them in the shadows.

"I don't know about you, but I could fly, Mr. Lavalier."

"Stay down here on the ground with me."

They managed to climb three stairs. It ended with a newel post pressing into her back, his knee bumping a spindle. When her hands explored the back of his thighs, roaming fearlessly higher, he got as hard as hardwood. "Hold it."

"I am," she murmured, a dreamy smile on her face.

"I meant stop that."

"Why, counselor, are you getting shy on me?"

"What I'm getting we need a bed for."

"We didn't yesterday."

Why'd she have to remind him of that? Brad grit his teeth and tried to think of bats and broomsticks instead of spells and love potions and voodoo for men lured to their doom by women with smiles like Carolina's and love-shining hazel eyes.

She nibbled his neck and got another moan from him.

"There was something else we didn't plan yesterday. Has to do with control."

"Self-control?"

He had little left to lose, and she was gleefully wresting that tiny bit away. "Birth control, sugar."

"Ah."

She might have fooled anyone else, but he knew she wasn't paying attention. That dare-anything glint in her eye said she was far more interested in seducing him than in thinking mundane, practical thoughts about preparation.

Which made it his responsibility. After all, it couldn't hurt for her to know that on rare occasions he was capable of common sense. What Carolina did next seemed designed to destroy every shred of it.

He caught his breath and stilled her hands. "I'm really sorry, darlin', give me five minutes."

"Is that all it'll take? I was thinking of a couple hours, at least."

"I mean to run back to the cottage. I left something there—"

It dawned slower than sunlight, but it did dawn. "You mean you left your, um, condoms at the cottage."

"These shorts don't have any pockets—"

She slowly withdrew her hands from right about where those pockets weren't. "You don't mean to tell me you went to Coulter's Pharmacy on your lunch hour?"

Brad had lived on the edge of the bayou long enough to sense a storm building. And too long in this town to be that dumb. "Slow down, 'Lina. I got 'em in Lafayette."

"When?"

"When I drove down to see the private investigator Saturday."

"But that was before—"

"A man can dream, can't he?"

And a woman can have the sense not to. "I want

this kept private." It was the only alternative between no love at all and being the talk of the town. "This is strictly between you and me."

"I don't plan on inviting anyone else along." He grinned, backing toward the door. "Back in five minutes. Trust me."

She did. Which was why she let him leave, let her steps carry her up that long, winding staircase to the bedroom with the lace and the four-poster bed. The emotional distance was greater, and yet the destination was as familiar as the X on a treasure map—an old family heirloom pointing the way.

She'd dreamed, but she'd never hoped. All her life she'd been surrounded by love. Gram's. Her parents'. Never her own. She'd made a life instead, striving for the things you could get by striving. Money. Success. Security. Love was shunted aside unless it could be controlled, guaranteed.

Finally Gram had called her home. To face the past, to make peace with the place where she belonged. It was time. Time to love a man without conditions and clauses. Time to learn what it really meant to be a Palmette.

Ten

The room glowed in gold as Carolina flicked on the bedside lamp. Withdrawing a stopper from a heart-shaped bottle, she dropped a bead of perfume on the bulb before it heated up. She slid a delicate pink scarf from a drawer and laid it over the light, roses over gold. Her trousseau.

"A true romantic," Brad said from the doorway.

"Gram was the romantic."

In a couple of steps he was beside her, his hand on the slope of her neck, tugging once at the shoulder of the sundress she wore.

"I didn't listen," she said softly.

He turned her without a word, gathering up her hair, running the zipper down. "Listen now." He ran a finger down the soft indentation of her spine, the teeth of the open zipper catching at him. The dress slid from her shoulders, landing on the floor with a whisper and a sigh.

"Something wrong?" she asked lightly, that devil-woman gleam back in her eye as she turned to him.

"If I'd known you weren't wearing anything under this dress, sugar, we'd still be on my sofa."

"A bed is better." She ran two hands down his front, then up again to curl around his neck, as if straightening a tie he could've sworn was choking him.

"Take off those shorts and we're even," she said.

He crushed her to him first. "You know how much sugar it takes to make alcohol?"

"I haven't the foggiest." It honestly didn't seem to matter, when she could make him catch his breath just by nipping his shoulder.

"It's intoxicating stuff. Makes a man lose his head."

She laughed at his chemistry lesson. He hated that. He was going to burst or do something stupid if she didn't stop being so damn beautiful. The Carolina he met in town was cool and reserved. Not his private lover.

He lifted her up and laid her back on the bed. The spread was dotted with white nubs he didn't care for. Not that he minded enough to do anything about them. "You want the sheets?"

He meant, did she want them turned down? Words weren't working right now and the only coherent thought she could manage were the concepts of care and tenderness, and those were about to go out the window too.

The first time they'd rushed, moving fast enough to catch dreams, overrun passion. He'd stopped short. He couldn't remember if she'd accepted his apology for that or not. He'd make it up to her now.

But every move she made said "faster," every gasp and sigh translated to "I want you." Her hair was a disheveled ebony halo, as tangled as their bodies. Both of them hot enough to hiss in the rain.

He wasn't going to let her get lost in passion, run away from what they were and what they were doing. There were consequences when a man and woman made love, commitments, silent or spoken.

She'd said she didn't want to love him. He was there to change her mind. The woman had already changed his life. "Love me, Carolina."

"I am, please . . ."

"Say it."

"I want you."

There hadn't been much to remove in the way of clothing. Naked, slick and ready, he stretched his body over hers, fighting the trembling in his forearms. He wasn't sure how much of that quaking was coming from her, but he could wait maybe a minute longer. "I need to hear it. Love me."

"I love you." She was asking.

He shook his head. "I love *you*. Tell me what you feel."

Him. Everywhere. Touching, reaching. She felt cherished, desired, overwhelmed—and totally in control. She moved under him and felt a distinct quiver in his limbs, akin to the final flimsy barrier between them. "Do you love me?"

"Yes," he insisted, willing to give to get.

"Show me."

She wrapped her legs around him. He sank inside. How could he not? The night was steamy, the bedroom close. Dragging in a breath was work. Sliding into Carolina was pure pleasure.

He stroked her, with his hands, his legs. He pressed kisses to each breast.

Her breath released in little gusts as he withdrew, sliding down her body, putting his mouth where his fingers found dew. Tasting honey.

"Oh Brad, I can't—"

She could. She was almost there, and he'd no more than touched her.

He took her rapidly to the stars, across light-years and time beyond measuring, through a waterfall of drenching, cleansing rain. She shuddered. Waves clenched, then rolled through her like the surface of the sea. Subsiding gradually, like the Gulf at dawn. He waited on the shore. "Still with me, love?"

She nodded, touching him blindly, running her hands over him, whispering wonders he hadn't shared. That was next—what they'd find together.

He slowly, slowly mounted her, aligning his body with hers, tucking her legs beneath them. He tasted a tear on the edge of her eyelash, took it in his mouth, inhaled the aroma of shampoo in midnight hair and held it to his heart. "Keep your legs under mine. This way."

He entered her then. The sensations were tight and hard, the motions small, the self-control almost unbearable until he felt it build in her all over again, until he got lost in the pounding throb of his own need, her quaking cries begging him to come with her. He would have followed her out on the balcony and up into the cold, empty heavens just to hear her call his name that way again.

"Oh babe." He groaned when the rockets dissolved in the sky.

"Hold me."

He intended to hold her forever. But minutes passed first, moments of mild words and tender promises. He slid out, kept her in his arms, and found a pillow she'd grasped from somewhere and dragged it alongside them. He nudged her to put her head on it too.

He wanted her to have room to breathe again, for the air to skim between them. And he wanted to stay just as they were.

They lay quiet until the sweat and the muggy night breeze cooled them.

She lifted his hand from her breast, kissing his fingers one by one. It wasn't an easy thing to say; it was the only thing. "I love you, Brad."

"You sure?"

She smiled, her tongue darting out to rake a fingertip. "Gram said I'd know when it was right."

"It wasn't right before?"

"No. No one. I was too busy protecting myself."

He didn't comment, didn't need to.

"Did you dream this too?"

"Night after night," he replied. "I thought you'd be the greatest woman in bed. Proved me wrong."

"What!" She sat up so fast, she might have been bitten by a killer bee.

He hauled her back to his side. "I never dreamed it would be this good, sugar. You wiped me out."

"That's more like it."

"Thank you. Feel free to do it again sometime."

"I just might." She pinched him, getting a startled grunt out of him. "What did you think of that stuff about the prenuptial agreement?"

"Getting some of this down in writing?"

"I'd like to hear it from you."

He stared at the rose-tinted lace draping the bed, wondering how hard it would be growing up taunted about illegitimacy, last of an infamous female line. The one time she'd taken control of her love life, it ended in ridicule. No wonder she abhorred scandal.

But she had him to protect her this time, to save her from scandal—and love her mightily at the same time.

He touched her again, the slope of her stomach, the flare of a hip, the soft weight of a breast. She was incomparably precious to him—and he wouldn't allow her to be insulted again. "Anyone so much as raises an eyebrow in your direction, sugar, you send 'em over to me. I don't care what people say."

Of course, in the long run, they'd all know. Marriage announcements and birth announcements spread like wildfire.

But that would have to come later. He was still working on hearing her say "I love you," on listening to her doubts crumble in softly spoken questions.

"What if I wanted guarantees?" she asked.

"I love you," he replied without hesitation. "I can't give you anything surer than that. But if you know me, that's all you need to know."

She chuckled softly.

"You laughin' at me?"

"It sounds so sweet and upright and honorable. I can just imagine you on Main Street at high noon waiting to have it out with some varmint over my honor."

"Damn right."

They laughed quietly, a breeze shuffling through the lace curtains.

"Seriously," she said after a few minutes.

"You would make a good lawyer."

"If there is such a thing."

"Uh-uh-uh. Careful now. I'm a whole lot bigger than you and meaner when provoked."

"I don't know about that." She carefully, devilishly plucked a hair from his chest. He yowled. "You still haven't answered my question."

"So it's torture, is it?"

"I want to know what you thought of the prenuptial agreement."

"Besides being terribly relieved you didn't marry the guy?"

He sat up, legs brushing hers on the nubby spread. He intended to answer her as soon as he swatted her on the rump and got her under the covers. But first he had to caress her ankle, then the knee beckoned, and before he knew it, he was probing the warmth between her thighs.

She lay on her side, a glow in her hazel eyes like embers of a fire that sparked back to life with the slightest encouragement. "Well?"

"I can't regret your checkered past when it led directly to our present." *Our future*, he didn't add just yet.

"What about your past? Romantically speaking." She squeezed her legs together, trapping his impertinent fingers.

"One serious, to-the-altar love affair."

"She leave you there?"

"Just about." He sighed, flopping down beside her in a blatant call for sympathy.

She nudged him playfully with her knee. "You couldn't have been too damaged. Get up. I want under the sheets now."

"How about under me? While we're at it, that is."

"Follow me and find out, sir." She pronounced it *suh*, slipping into a drawl as thick as the fragrance of honeysuckle through the windows. "Come on ovah hyeah."

"Since you were kind enough to ask . . ."

Sounds surrounded them, deep bullfrog notes from the edge of the bayou, resounding over the fields, leaves and grass and whispering wind, a creaking bed, a sighing curtain. Laughter, sudden and delighted, joined the chorus—and a yip and a love bite, panted pleasures and murmured words. Nothing was private now, even when a hand emerged from the rumpled cotton and flicked off the light. Blackness settled around them, the night noises resumed, and the loving didn't stop.

Brad showed her how to take love slow, luxuriating in the simmering night, flames fed by body heat, glowing scarlet embers that met the crimson dawn.

"Where are you going?" he asked.

"I said I'd be at the brokerage at eight this morning. When do you get up, Mr. Lavalier?"

He stretched, his chest expanding, his long arms knocking the walnut headboard. He pulled himself up to a half-sitting position, hair disheveled, jaw sooty with morning beard, and a look in his eye that said she wasn't going anywhere just yet.

His hand circled her wrist loosely as she traipsed by the bed. "I get up, pumpkin, whenever I think, speak, or hear your name. Any more foolish questions?"

Her brow was still furrowed, and her mouth twisted as if she'd bitten a lemon. "Pumpkin?" She dragged a wisp of lacy underthings from the night-stand and stepped into them. "Pumpkin?"

"Would you prefer Love Goddess of the Dark?"

"I like that *much* better."

And she loved him—more deeply, more freely, more openly than she'd thought possible. One night in each other's arms and a lifetime of barriers were laid waste. Part of her wondered how she'd escaped this all her life, the other part wondered why. It didn't matter now, the doubts evaporating in air too muggy to evaporate anything else.

"How about a shower?" she suggested, a glimmer in her eye as she pinned up her hair.

"You are insatiable!"

"And who woke up with"—she tiptoed her fingers up his thigh—"with me this morning?"

"The one man crazy enough to take on a cursed woman."

"But if I'm in love with you, you must be my curse. Oh dear."

"Try 'oh my.'"

And she did. When he nipped her arm, kissed her neck, and did things to her flesh she hadn't thought possible. Twenty minutes later she was breathless, damp, and panting for air.

"Did you say something about a shower?" he asked, looking about as unlikely a candidate for movement as she.

"I, ah, I—"

"Take your time, 'Lina."

She laughed again. Was going to bed with a man supposed to be so much fun? It certainly offset the scarier emotions; so did the way he turned her inside out, expecting her to reveal sides of her soul no woman revealed, unless absolute trust was there.

"I think," she began slowly, hoping the pattern in the lace bed curtains would come into focus half as clearly as his twinkling gaze, "I think I was asking what time you get out of bed."

"Probably three seconds after you do." He propped

his head on his hand and looked down at her wide-eyed expression.

"You're not proposing chasing me to the bathroom too?"

No, but proposing might not be a bad idea, he thought. It generally came somewhere after "I love you." Speaking of which, he'd only said it four times while they'd made love—before he lost count. "I love you."

She smiled, a shy, pleased smile, as if for a moment she'd forgotten, or feared he had. "I love you too."

"Maybe we can stay here and discuss this further." His fingertip made lazy circles on her skin. There was some kind of pulse beat next to her navel. He counted to five.

"You have to go to work."

"Mmm." Seven. Eight.

"You can't be late, Brad."

She wasn't teasing now. There was that small off-center crease of worry between her brows.

"Don't want me sauntering into the office with a smile plastered on my face, is that it?" He shook his head before she could speak, her face cupped in his palm. "I know. Your terms were privacy. Just you and me. That's it for now."

And the day after, or the day after that, or the week after, they'd go public. They'd have to when she began wearing his ring. An emerald, to match her eyes, ruby for her fire, onyx for bedrock family loyalty, and opal for the shimmer in her eyes when she looked at him.

"Brad?" Both her hands firmly lifted his face from where he'd taken to suckling a sensitive nipple with his lips. "What time do you have to be at work?"

"Nine o'clock."

Her head fell back on the pillow. "What a woman has to do to get a straight answer around here!"

• • •

The laughter followed her through the morning. And the touches. And the little aches signaling that her body hadn't been quite so completely and totally made use of in years.

And her heart, never.

She spent a solid three hours at the brokerage firm. A man in a white suit walked by the plate window, and her heart skittered, leaving her wondering what medical science made of all this. Hearts didn't usually soar, did they? Did that show on an EKG, making rainbow arcs on the graph paper?

Her heart beat double time when "BrD $6\frac{3}{4}$" scanned by on the readout. It was going up, a good buy.

"If you aren't getting superstitious!" her conscience declared.

She excused herself for an eleven o'clock hair appointment at Tête-á-Tête. The bounce in Carolina's step leveled out as she neared the front door, across the street and three doors down from Brad's. Grelick-ville's gossip headquarters posed as a beauty salon.

If Shepherd had put anything about her and Brad on the grapevine, the ladies there would know. She took a deep breath and went in.

"Meggy-Sue," the receptionist called, "you come on out here and see who's come over."

"If it ain't Carolina Palmette. Well, hello, darlin'. You certainly been keepin' your distance, child."

Carolina patted her hair, reduced all over again to the young woman who'd raced out of there determined never to show her face in town again. But despite the curious looks the ladies exchanged, she caught no knowing winks. "I didn't really need a cut until now. It's been almost six weeks since I—"

"No harm, honey. You just come on over here to the sink, and we'll do you up fine. Rhonda? Whyn't you pour our Carolina a drink here."

Four small glasses of sherry glittered like liquid rubies on a silver tray. Carolina had forgotten the civilized tradition, but not its way of loosening the tongue. She wished she could forget the aftertaste of moonshine. But it was too mixed up with the taste of Brad.

"You don't want any?" Meggy-Sue's eager expression sank.

"How could I say no to this? You all make me feel right at home."

Relieved smiles blossomed all around.

That's when it dawned on her. They'd expected her to turn them down, to reject their hospitality and them with it. As if her distance hadn't been self-protection but a judgment on them.

"I was afraid of what you thought of *me*," she almost said, unsure how to communicate that. Only aware that she wanted to tell Brad about it, that the people in her hometown hadn't rejected her as she'd feared all these years. That maybe it was time to move back, grapevine and all.

But there was no framing an apology while the hair dryers hummed and fresh gossip flowed, familiar as Gram's own voice. It was the current of a river she'd lived beside all her life. They pampered her and petted her and, yes, questioned her mercilessly, but she didn't mind. They wanted to know, not judge; they wanted to be part of her life.

And if she stayed in Grelickville, they would be.

"Oh, look at the time!" Twelve-thirty already, and she had phone calls to make, clients to talk to. "Let it air dry, Meggy."

"Let me braid this last part, hon. Them stocks will wait."

"But there's lunch too."

"With Brad Lavalier?"

A half dozen smiles suddenly turned her way, including those under the dryers who couldn't have possibly heard. Her open and generous feelings suddenly shriveled like a raisin. Yes, she loved them all and saw that in their hearts they were good, but that didn't mean she was ready to unburden her love life to them.

Neither was she going to hide.

Her answer carried to every ear in Tête-á-Tête. "Yes, I'm having lunch with Brad."

"We all heard you had a *late* lunch yesterday. Charlene was in here—"

"—having her roots done—"

"—and none too soon, you ask me—"

"—saying she'd seen you two having quite a close conversation."

"We were discussing the case." Among other things.

"I bet that lawyer's easy to work with, ain't he?"

"Very." Carolina managed to smile, withdraw the proper amount from her wallet, and ease her way toward the door. She wondered if mad, passionate sex did anything for the condition of a woman's hair. Meggy-Sue had already remarked on her heightened coloring and how prettily those gold specks in her eyes glistened.

"Afternoon, now."

"Afternoon, hon. Stop on back when you got some time to talk."

"I will." She bumped her knee on the bell strip and skedaddled, almost bumping into Brad as she hopped the curb.

"Mornin'," he said, voice so low, a deep inner part of her thrummed in reply.

"Afternoon, I think."

"You look as if you're in a hurry."

She had been. Now she couldn't seem to move. The collar button she was eye-to-eye with reminded her of the chest beneath, the throat behind, and the wide, welcoming mouth above. "Maybe you'd better not hold me like this."

Brad sent a brief glance to the window of Tête-á-Tête and the ladies brazenly watching the show. He gripped Carolina's shoulders, lifted her heels an inch off the ground, and set her just as firmly back down. "Watch those curbs now."

"I will."

"Good."

He unbuttoned the one button holding his suit coat closed, then sank his hands deep in the pockets of his loose pleated pants, for a second pulling them taut over the hard ridge behind the zipper. No one but Carolina saw, but when he licked his lips, rockets went off through her central nervous system. If she'd been wired to the New York Stock Exchange, there'd be a crash for sure. "Charlene reported the kiss in the restaurant."

He made a show of being deep in thought. "Oh yes. The good-bye kiss."

"Don't pretend you don't remember."

He shrugged suavely and said, "There've been so many since."

Her color was high enough without him adding to it. "If we're keeping this private, it can't happen again."

To her surprise, and a flickering pang of regret, he agreed instantly.

"I promise I won't ever kiss you good-bye again."

She had no idea how much he meant that. He'd been doing a lot of thinking. Long-term. Short-term. Whenever he got his mind off the night before or the night to come, he thought about what kind of future they could have. None of it included saying good-bye.

And so, proper as a Boy Scout, he touched the back of her elbow and led her across the street. Since noontime traffic consisted of approximately eight cars, and they'd already passed by, he stopped dead in the center of Bayou Street. "Of course, that doesn't rule out a kiss hello."

With one arm around her back, he bent her parallel to the pavement and proceeded to kiss her right out of her shoes.

Eleven

"Brad Lavalier, after that shameful display you put on at lunch, I don't know if I'll ever kiss you again." Carolina rolled over in bed, working on a pout that would do Scarlett O'Hara proud. She wrapped a totally unnecessary sheet around her and stalked out on the balcony.

"Whatever you say," he drawled, watching her fanny sway.

"Hmmph!" She swished the sheet behind her like Lady Di's wedding train.

"Darlin', you've done just about everything a woman can do to a man short of mouth-to-mouth resuscitation. I'd be selfish to want kisses too."

"Lord knows you're selfish enough as it is. Kissin' me in the middle of Bayou Street! You completely ignored my desire to keep this quiet."

"One," he counted, voice firm and low as he came up behind her, fingers ticking off his reasons as he wrapped his arms around her waist, "I keep track of each and every one of your desires. Two, I love the way your accent comes back when you're angry, sugar. And three, Charlene already told half the town about yesterday's kiss."

"So you demonstrated for those who missed it?"

She wasn't half as mad as she pretended—that fiery temper was part of the game. She knew, and he knew, he'd sooner plunge through the creaky porch roof below than cause her pain.

He studied the back of her head, figuring which row went where in the intricate braid and how it all held together, marveling at the way it stayed in place. Meggy-Sue must be an engineering wonder, considering the love he and Carolina had been making since he'd dropped in for dinner. The bottle of wine and bucket of shrimp were long gone, and only one tantalizing strand of her hair had snuck out of place.

"What did they really see, 'Lina? A kiss is just a kiss."

"And 'a sigh is just a sigh'?"

It was when he held her to his chest. He kissed the dusky shadowed skin behind her ear, watching the moon rise over the cottage. "Keep humming, sugar. You and I are going to make music, and babies, and—"

"And talk."

"And love."

"Again?"

"Again."

It was much later when she tapped him on the chest, ruthlessly waking him from what promised to be a most pleasant dream. "Brad."

"Hmm?"

"Guess who the reverend's courting now?"

"Sugar, can't we talk it over in the morning? I don't want him in bed with us."

"Neither do I. But listen. He's after Dotty Willis and the money Gram left her."

"I know that. I was here when y'all talked about it."

"But he's also pestering Marjorie Sams. *And* Belinda Bates."

"Promising them what?" He was awake now, body still thrumming, eyes gritty but open.

"He wants them to withdraw their life savings and give to his church."

"In cash?"

She loved the way his abdomen rippled when he sat up.

"Where'd you hear all this, 'Lina?"

"I get my hair cut at Tête-à-Tête; you don't. That's a serious disadvantage your private detective's going to have. It's where all the information is."

"And Belinda and Marjorie?"

"Belinda offered the reverend use of her late husband's Cadillac, but he suggested she sell it and give him the money instead. Belinda's hesitating; she's mighty attached to that car."

"And Marjorie?"

"He had one of those gorilla assistants of his go over to her house and talk to her about donating the money now rather than leaving it to him in her will."

"What'll she live on?"

"A lifetime annuity from his church."

"And that'll dry up the minute he crosses the state line."

"What do you think?"

"I think he's getting ready to skip and take everything that isn't tied down."

"Like the land."

"Like the land."

She touched him tenderly. "I love you."

"Love you too," he murmured, still thinking.

"I ought to thank you for saving Gram's land. Among other things."

"I haven't yet."

"But he can't take it with him, can he? And if he leaves, it's mine." She propped herself up on an elbow, fixing him with a troubled look. "But what about your other clients? We can't have him running off with their savings?"

She'd gone from fighting her own battles to helping him fight his. He skimmed the satiny side of her breast with the back of his fingers. "You're a generous-hearted woman, Carolina. I knew you had it in you."

"It took me a while to realize how much I hurt other people by protecting myself. I'm sure I hurt my fiancé by asking for his love in writing."

Brad grimaced and heaved an exaggerated sigh. "I don't want him in bed with us either."

"Now who's the selfish one? Jealous too." She grinned, tickling him until he pinned her hands and drew her down beside him again.

They settled in for a long, quiet night. Brad stared out at the stars, his mind retreating to the first time he'd met Carolina, what she'd needed, what he'd promised. "It's going to be hard to catch Shepherd and keep it quiet too. If we prosecute, people will have to come forward. You're not the only one who's proud. People don't like looking gullible." As he once had.

"If it comes down to my privacy or somebody's life savings, I'll understand."

"Easy to say when we're snuggled in bed," he teased, recognizing she was getting braver all the time when it came to facing the people of Grelickville. He wasn't. He didn't want to risk what they'd gained. Maybe it would be better to keep this secret—their own private affair. Maybe Shepherd would move on and there would be no courtroom scenes, no headlines.

Heck, he thought with a dry laugh, Grelickville didn't even had a newspaper.

"We'll confront him quietly and with a minimum of fuss," he murmured. "Tomorrow."

He tucked her in beside him, wanting her next to him as they slept. Carolina curled up close. It wasn't the newness of having someone to love that filled her with a sweet ache, it was the familiar way he did it. It was as if they'd been married for years, talking over the events of the day, mulling the latest gossip, plotting out a future.

Could marriage really be so easy? Could her whole world change and yet come down to something as simple as this home? This man? Down the road, years from now, would that quiver always begin, intense and low like the vibrations of a cello bow drawn across strings, when his fingers played down her back, his breath stirring her hair?

She draped an arm over his chest. Long after his breathing became slow and even, she lay awake thinking. "Thank you, Gram," she whispered.

The phone rang so far off, she had to be dreaming it. As she stirred, her body reminded her of the hundred and one ways Brad had explained how he loved her the previous night. Shepherd was quickly forgotten.

Another ring startled her awake. She fumbled the receiver to her ear. "Hello?"

She looked at the clock. It wasn't there, or rather Brad was, the clock blocked by his shoulder. His hand rested on her thigh, heavy and male and reassuring. A smile crooked his mouth even in sleep.

Maybe it was because a recumbent woman, flush with similar dreams, was crawling over him to see the time. "Hello?"

A man's voice crackled in panic. "Is Lavalier there? Get me Lavalier, please."

Instantly, Carolina was awake enough to know better. "This is the Palmette house."

"I'm at the jail. It's an emergency, he's got to come. He lives out there, don't he?"

Carolina shook Brad's shoulder, hoping he'd wake up without asking why or who or what time it was.

"There's no answer at his cottage," the man hurried on. "Could you tell me where he's gone?"

"I'm sorry, Mr. . . ." No name was forthcoming, no doubt due to the caller's agitated state. By now Brad was awake.

Grabbing a pillow, he stuffed it between the back of his head and the headboard. He fingered the lace edging of the short camisole Carolina had pulled on during the night, as if wondering where it had come from.

It wasn't necessary on a hot night, but she'd never had anyone to wear it for. She'd hoped, when they awoke . . .

"Did he go out of town? You have any idea where he might be?"

"He jogs some mornings, perhaps if you call his house in fifteen minutes." She prodded Brad with her foot, and he nodded in resignation, planting a kiss on her arm as he got up.

"They won't let me have another call."

"Oh. If you give me your name, I could leave him a message to go straight to the jail." She enunciated that last part for Brad.

"Do not pass Go," he muttered, pulling on his pants. "Do not collect two hundred dollars."

The voice grew considerably huskier, choking back emotion. "Look, if he doesn't get down here, I don't know what I'll do. I have to be to work. I'll be fired this time if I ain't. The whole town'll know, the scandal, my wife—"

Carolina knew all about scandal. She lifted the phone off the end table and walked it as far as the line would stretch. "Sir? Hold on a minute. He'd be happy to help you."

She handed Brad the phone.

He covered the receiver, looking in hazel eyes where pride and compassion mixed. "You sure?"

"I don't know who he is, but he's in trouble."

Brad would have kissed her if there'd been time. "Remind me to tell you I love you." He cleared the morning gravel out of his throat. "This is Brad Lavalier."

The line went dead.

• • •

It could have been a bad connection. The man was clearly agitated. Brad would settle it when he got down to the jail. Carolina knew she really shouldn't worry. But for some reason, the call dogged her all day.

Brad called briefly at lunchtime about some faxes from the private detective. There was a revival meeting that night. He might have enough to confront Shepherd after the service.

"*We* might have enough," she corrected.

" 'Lina, I promised us both I'd keep this discreet as possible and not drag you into it. You stay home."

"And bake cookies and shoofly pie? Think again, counselor. This is my home I'm defending."

"Our home."

The instant rejoinder buzzed as loud as the interference on the portable phone she'd carted into the dining room. "Ours?" she said sweetly.

"We'll talk later," Brad said.

"Yes, we will."

She set down the receiver, uttering a quick, lady-like curse. "You forgot to ask him about that man at the jail."

He'd tell her when he got home.

Home.

Carolina knew things weren't settled yet between them, but they looked better all the time. "Gram, you may have a wedding in this house yet."

The pounding on the door had Carolina rushing from the kitchen, glancing at the time, and laughing at her own exhilaration. She hadn't cooked dinner for a man in ages. She flung open the door. "This is crazy. Oh!"

"Crazy is right, child," Dotty said, bustling past her into the hall. "That man is going to drive me out of my mind!"

"Who?"

"The reverend, who else? He's done pleaded with me and pleaded with me. Sign this. Donate that."

Carolina followed as Dotty made straight for the kitchen and took down two glasses for iced tea. "Sit."

She sat.

"That young man of yours might chase a woman right out of her skin, but believe me I'd take lawyers over preachers any day. Claimin' God on their side as if they run a tollbooth to Him. If that man's holy, I'm Dolly Parton!"

"What did he say?"

"I'll tell you when he gets here."

"You invited the reverend here?"

"No, child, your young lawyer."

At that moment a loud male voice reverberated through the front hall. "Pumpkin, I'm home!"

Carolina stared at Dotty, a smile frozen to her face.

"Huh!" Dotty went back to scoping out the refrigerator. "He's gonna give us some advice, pumpkin."

Dotty's cackle trailed Carolina as she scurried down the hall. She had to catch Brad before he did something crazy like shed all his clothes on the way back to greet her. "Dotty's here."

He insisted on kissing her first. Thoroughly. "Kisses are already public, remember?"

Not those kisses. He had her pulse tick-tocking like a time bomb by the time he set her down. She caught her breath and took him firmly by the hand. "You're coming into the kitchen and you're behaving."

"Of course I am, pumpkin."

"And don't call me pumpkin!"

"Evenin', Dotty."

Dotty was muttering over an unidentifiable foodstuff in a plastic container. "If y'all have anything fresh in this house, I can feed you while we talk."

"Thank you, Dotty. We'd be mighty obliged if you would." Brad pulled out a kitchen chair. "Have a seat, 'Lina."

Before she could take it, he scooted in under her,

capturing her on his lap. "To what do we owe the honor, Dotty?"

"That reverend's about to drive me outta my mind. You'd think he was headwaiter at the Pearly Gates, slip him a few thousand and he'll get you a table nearer God."

"Thousand?" Brad's voice lowered quickly, his gaze intent, his arms wrapped securely around Carolina's middle.

"Ten thousand. Every penny Eve Palmette left me. Said if I gave it to him in cash, he'd invest it. With a little help from the church, I could live off the proceeds comfortably for the rest of my life. I tell you I don't trust a man who wears prettier rings than I do."

"Did you sign anything?" Brad asked.

Dotty lifted her imposing bosom and lowered her chin to look over it. "Boy, if you got no better sense than to ask me that question, I don't know what I'm talkin' to you for."

Brad exchanged a shamed glance with Carolina, who smothered a smile. "Sorry, Dotty."

Carolina stopped squirming on Brad's lap. "When he talked about investments, did he guarantee you any return on your money?"

"He said he's a-going to build a church bigger than Calvary Baptist. It'll serve half this parish and the next. Says all the new members will contribute, and I'll be paid back out of their money. A pool, he calls it."

"Sounds more like a pyramid to me." Carolina looked at Brad. "If he's talking investment instead of donations, we've got him."

"How?"

"Pyramid schemes are illegal. You can give away all the money you want, but investments are governed by rules and regulations."

"And laws."

She squeezed Brad's hand. "And laws. By George, I think we've got him."

• • •

"Don't know what it was in that supper, but I got a flock of butterflies starting up that could float the Goodyear blimp." Brad patted his abdomen as they stood at the back of the revival tent, people filing past.

"Maybe you need a drink."

"From an angel?" he asked, eyeing the closest he'd ever come to one.

"You remembered," she teased. "As I recall, you're nervous speaking to groups."

"I don't plan on speaking to this one. We'll go to Shepherd's trailer when the meeting is over. If he returns the money he's gained and leaves quietly, the land is yours."

"Meanwhile, we stand right here and make sure he doesn't skip town."

"You got it."

Carolina raised herself up on tiptoe and whispered in his ear. "I've got you, counselor. And no woman was ever happier."

Or lovelier. Brad's gaze traveled the length of the formfitting dress she wore. Elegant, white and spare, it would appear icy and sleek to a man who was easily intimidated. To him it was sexy and sassy, like the woman inside it. It shone on her. Love did too. And he was proud as a knight in polished armor that she was his. "You're holding my hand for all to see, sugar."

"It's just a hand." She shrugged playfully.

"With a heart attached. It's all yours, Carolina."

"Ours," she said simply, kissing him softly on the lips this time. Yes, she had come a long way. All the way home to the love Gram had promised. Next time she got him alone, she had some promises of her own to make.

"See any openings, Lavalier?" a latecomer asked.

Brad scanned the tent for empty seats, easily shak-

ing hands or patting the backs of those still filing in.
He looked like a mild country lawyer on the surface,
lanky and handsome and rumpled.

The man can't keep a suit pressed to save his life,
Carolina thought with a smile. But she noticed how
his gaze turned to steel when Shepherd took the
stage. Only a city slicker or a fool would underesti-
mate him. Carolina hoped the reverend was a bit of
each.

She tapped Brad on the wrist. "Still nervous?"

"I'm ready to saddle up that horse now," he
drawled. "But I need something from you."

"What is it?"

"A lady used to give her knight a scarf or a handkerchief to take with him into battle."

She adopted her deepest southern belle accent.
"I'm afraid I left mine at home, suh."

"I'd settle for that slip of lace you were wearing this
morning."

"I'll have to hand it to you later."

His eyes darkened as his grin spread. "Promise?"

"Oh yes."

The microphone screeched and settled into a distinct hum. The reverend took a deep breath, eyes
darting to the back of the tent, where Brad and
Carolina stood side by side. "The text of this evening's
sermon will be 'We Are All Sinners.' But first, friends,
Ah'm going to be leaving you soon."

Brad squeezed her hand.

She smiled. "Here he goes."

Other murmurs met his announcement, agitated
paper fans swatted at the air.

"You see, people, I have a confession to make. I've
been guilty. Guilty of pride. I thought I could do the
Lord's work alone."

"He's covering his tracks," Carolina whispered to
Brad.

"Face-saving. Just as long as he returns the money
and goes."

"Friends," the speakers rumbled the reverend's words, "there are people who will try to accuse me of many things in the coming days. You see 'em back there now, lurking by the entrance to our place of worship."

All heads turned.

Brad's mouth went dry. This wasn't the way he wanted to play it; there was no choice now. "We can talk about this later, Reverend."

"I have nothing to hide from this congregation, son. Accuse me as you will."

Every fan stopped and every chair creaked. In seconds, Carolina and Brad were being scrutinized by every eye in the place. Even the organist stood up to get a better look.

Brad released Carolina's hand. A little too late. They'd all seen.

No matter. He cleared his throat, taking three leisurely steps up the aisle. He always thought better on shoe leather. "I have evidence," he announced to the crowd, "from towns as far away as the Florida panhandle, Alabama, Mississippi. This man has left a path of betrayed trust behind him wider than Sherman's march through Georgia."

The crowd rumbled with "no's" and scattered denials.

Brad knew then he should have done this a long time ago. By now people were hooked. A congregation of believers objected to being told they'd been played for fools.

Shepherd soothed the hisses and the few outraged shouts, brushing the microphone with his lips to mutter one scornful word. "Evidence?"

"From a private detective."

"Hear that, friends? They're coming after me with detectives now."

There were more angry murmurs. The mood was rapidly turning ugly. Carolina shivered as if touched by ice. Brad knew these people. She watched him make eye contact with ones she recognized too. They'd listen. They had to.

"His usual method is selling church-building bonds," Brad shouted. "Or lifetime annuities."

A few startled cries confirmed the charges. More than one person had heard those promises.

"This time his methods changed," Brad added, dropping his voice, forcing them to listen close. "Thanks to Eve Palmette, he found himself tied down to land. He had to stick around. He couldn't run with the money quite so fast."

"Theories and spurious accusations," Shepherd announced. "Fancy words alongside his fancy lady. Don't she look pretty there? Step forward, honey. You're part of this, too, I believe."

It was a diversion, plain and simple. Carolina froze, tilting her chin up slightly out of sheer habit. She stood her ground.

"The lady has nothing to do with this," Brad interjected. "This is about fraud. Misrepresentation. Selling false securities—"

"Excuse me, son, but it's about her grandmother's land. Land this church has been blessed with." Shepherd's voice rose with every word. He might not have right on his side, but he had four hundred-watt speakers on either side of his stage. "I say that young lady has had her head turned by this shoestring no-account lawyer from New Orleans. He came to this little town just looking to stir up trouble and drum up business!"

Brad charged down the aisle toward Shepherd until he was at the foot of the stage. He wouldn't have the spotlight turned on Carolina. Shouting himself hoarse, he repeated the charges, hauling crumpled faxes from the private detective out of his suit pockets. "Names! Dates! Amounts! Old women left with nothing to live on but the charity of their children. Don't let it happen here!"

The crowd was on its feet, hurling wadded paper fans at Shepherd, at Brad, jeering and cursing.

The reverend hushed the melee with a wave of his hand. Heads turned back to him once more, faces lifted. "I admit," he said softly, "I've been wrong."

A wave of murmurs rustled through the congregation like wind through a wheat field.

"I've been too trusting, friends, too proud. I ignored their innuendos, their doubts and defamations. Until this moment, when I am forced to carry this burden. I ask only for my day of judgment."

"You'll get that in a court of law," Brad vowed.

The reverend looked down from his pulpit. "I was appealing to a higher court, young man."

A handful of "Amen's" sounded under the tent.

He'd walked right into that one, Brad thought.

"Before I descend this stage and submit to your persecution, son, I ask only one question."

Brad squared his shoulders, folding the faxes in his hand. It had been messy, it had been public. But the battle was almost won. "Ask it."

Shepherd frowned, as if sincerely pained by the question at hand. He dramatically looked to heaven, scanning the seams of the tent, the string of lights, the woman standing at the end of the aisle, white dress outlined against the black night outside.

Brad followed the man's gaze, his heart suddenly too heavy to beat.

In the thick evening air, the amplified words echoed through the tent. "Tell me, son, whose bed were you sleeping in at five o'clock this mornin'?"

Twelve

The hush swallowed up everything. An overhead fan quietly sliced the air to ribbons.

Carolina couldn't breathe. She crossed her arms over her middle, trapping a sob that threatened to escape from somewhere deep inside her. That emergency telephone call earlier that morning had been a setup. Shepherd's suspicions were confirmed, and it was her fault.

Brad stood silent, rooted to the dusty ground. He'd lost whatever case could be made. The mortified look on Carolina's face told him he'd lost a lot more than that.

He'd promised to defend the woman, instead he'd dragged her with him, wanting her beside him all the way. What a fool he'd been. Shepherd's kind of scum played hardball. Who else would be heartless enough to swindle old people of everything they had? Did Brad think the man would run because of a few accusations?

"Well, son?"

If he didn't say it, Shepherd would, and in decidedly uglier terms. "I was in the bed of the woman I love."

"Is that your answer?" Shepherd purred into the

microphone, eager to pronounce judgment to the hundred-man jury.

A judgment that snake had no right to make, Carolina thought as a sudden fury ripped through her like canvas snapping in a high wind, wind that howled and hurt the way she did. But it wouldn't stop her from going to Brad's side. "That's the truth," she called out.

Her legs unlocked and she strode down the aisle, two bright spots of color shining on her cheeks, otherwise as pale as sawdust. She linked her arm through Brad's for all to see. "It's true," she announced calmly, turning in each direction. "But that doesn't change the fact that this man is a crook."

She looked out at the sea of faces. It was easier than looking at Brad. She needed his strength to lean on, to stand beside. She needed to know he loved her, and that's all she needed. But if he so much as squeezed her hand, she feared she'd break in a million pieces.

He thought he could fight off a snake like Shepherd with something as paltry as evidence. But this was the court of public opinion, of beliefs and appearances and snap judgments. Where preachers were good and lawyers bad. Where love was as suspect as the gift of an apple from the original Eve.

"I love this man," she said, holding his hand tight, her voice shaking as she pushed it to reach the farthest corners of the tent. "Maybe we were wrong to love too much, but I'm a Palmette. And that's the way we do things."

Walking down a country road in the moonlight should have been romantic. Brad felt as if he were walking in front of a firing squad. She still hadn't looked him in the eye.

She'd held his arm until they'd cleared the tent, taking his hand as they wended their way through the parked cars. But the minute they reached the road leading to the last ten acres of Palmette land, she let go.

He dropped back a step and watched her walk. A pale ghost, another kind of dream shattered.

Dammit, he'd ruined her life. The least she could do was look at him.

They walked past the house without speaking, shoes clicking on the seashell drive, insects singing in the lush dark. The distant drone of a hymn wafted over the fields from the revival.

She stepped up on the back porch, where a light burned. "You coming in?"

"No." The word almost didn't make it out of his mouth.

Her eyes were tear-bright, her cheeks resolutely dry. He saw no vulnerability in her now, no fear. She was wrapped up tight in the cloak of pride she'd worn when he'd first met her, protector of the family honor.

She might be cool and collected, he was half out of his mind with worry and the bitter taste of self-condemnation. Shepherd couldn't begin to call him the names he called himself.

"Maybe I should stay out here."

"Too late for secrets now," she said. "Come in. Have some tea."

She was smiling! They'd just had their relationship flaunted in front of a hundred Holy Rollers, and she had the nerve to smile. "No. But you're right on one thing, we can't hide in there anymore."

"Shall we go around to the front door, then? Walk in there?"

He got it now. She was pretending everything was normal, that he hadn't botched it completely. She silently defied him to say otherwise, just as she'd defied the audience. He could barely guess what it cost her to face them all and admit to being what everyone expected. Just another Palmette.

He knew what it cost him. Just as he'd done after Pearl River, he had to make a gesture. It might be late, but he had to make it all the same. He wouldn't make her kick him out. "Let me do the dirty work here. There's a room at Mrs. Boudrine's. She's taking in boarders. I'll go there until things blow over."

"It's a little late to pretend we're only neighbors."

He probably thought that was funny, coming from her. For Carolina it was too painfully ironic; suddenly Brad was the one worried about appearances. The man who'd almost taken her in the rain. Who whispered the most delicious, tempting, bone-thrilling things. Who joked in bed and muttered in his sleep. The man she loved more than all the world was now determined to stay as far away from her as possible.

"Don't look at me that way," he said, turning to glare at the knowing wink of tent lights over the flat land. "This is all my fault."

"And who picked up the phone this morning? Who handed it over? Can we blame you for that too?"

"Yes." Because he'd loved her more for her compassion. He'd kissed her as some kind of reward. She'd been so brave.

She was acting brave now. Looking at him as if *she* hurt for *him*. Brad bit back a shot of acid. "The one thing you asked me to do when we first met was keep this quiet. I promised you I would."

"You promised me a lot of things."

She laid her hand over his on the railing. "But moving won't solve anything. I tried it, remember?" When she got no answer, she folded her hands lightly in front of her. There was another possibility, another reason he might want to put distance between them. "Are you ashamed? Does loving me embarrass you? I wasn't the only one stared at tonight."

The fiery look in his eye almost made her quail. "I'm ashamed of letting the woman I love be dragged through the mud. Mud she warned me about in advance." He cupped her face with his hand, for a brief moment looking gentle, looking tired. "Good try. But you won't convince me you weren't scared. I saw the look on your face when he asked."

"Well, yes." She laughed dryly, crossing her arms, wanting so much to be held and somehow unable to ask. "It isn't easy watching your worst nightmare come true. I may be a little the worse for wear, but I'm a Palmette. I've dealt with this all my life, one way or another. We can deal with it now."

We. He started to speak, to halt her lightly spoken monologue.

She stopped him with three cool fingertips pressed to his lips. "No, Brad, I'm right. Gram was right. I love you and that's all that matters in this world. The rest is just talk."

"Then why did you look as if someone had just punched you in the gut?"

"Because you were trying so hard to defend me, and I didn't know what to do."

"Trying and failing. Knights don't drag their ladies onto the battlefield with them. You should have stayed here."

"And hide? As I recall, Sir Knight, you said you were in the bed of the woman you love this morning. Didn't a king use those words once?"

"You know the name of DeVoe's mangy dog? King."

She laughed and shook her head. "Oh no you don't. No self-pity. You were my hero back there." She wrapped her arms around his neck, eyes alight with fire. "And when you said you loved me in front of all those people, I was the proudest woman in the world. Proud to be fighting at your side."

He kissed her, hard. She wanted him to. He opened her lips and tasted her sweet heat, her laughter, a salty trace of tears that had never fallen. The words came tumbling out, fast and harsh and desperate. "Then marry me, dammit. As soon as possible. We'll stop all the talk right now."

"No."

Her answer rocked him softly back on his heels. " 'Lina, look at me."

She did, pride burning as fierce as ever in her gaze. Strokes of color slashed across her cheekbones. Flashes of anger and pain he didn't understand. "Making a decent woman of me, Brad?"

"Don't talk crazy."

"Who's concerned about what people think now?"

"Aren't you?"

"Not anymore." It was honest, it was deep, and it was no use. She loved him despite the talk, the rumors, the scandal. She'd lost so many years of her life to worrying what the people of Grelickville thought, to avoiding love. She wasn't giving them her future too.

"Then the answer's no," he said bluntly. "I'll move what I can out of the cottage and be gone by morning."

She knew Dotty thought she'd flipped, wanting to do canning on such a hot day, but she had to keep busy or go mad. The house sparkled from top to bottom. The days dragged. The nights were long and silent. The cottage empty.

Shepherd was gone, tent, trailer, and folding chairs. Evidence hadn't done it; the grapevine had. Once word got around about Brad's accusations and people compared stories, Shepherd was history.

And Carolina was downright amused to find her scandalous behavior the *second* most talked-about subject in town.

She went into Grelickville every day. Purposely, restlessly, visiting the brokerage, the grocery, Tête-á-Tête. Wednesday's visit cost her three inches off her hair. But if stories were going to circulate about her and Brad, she was determined to tell their version.

"Our two cents' worth," she murmured, stirring a pot of bubbling blueberries. They'd make good pies this winter. Nothing like a home-baked pie. She glanced around the kitchen. Nothing like a home. "Dotty?"

"Yes, child?"

"Remember when I was little and kids used to tease me about Mom and Pop?"

"Yes, I do. You held your head up real high, though, like Mizz Palmette taught you."

"People acted as if I should be ashamed. But they loved each other. I didn't see what there was to be ashamed of."

"No reason you should, child. Love burns hot around here. Think folks would know that by now."

"But eventually I learned to be ashamed. And it took me a long time to unlearn that." It took Brad Lavalier. "He doesn't seem to realize that I've realized it's okay to love."

"You lost me there, child."

"Brad thinks my life was somehow ruined when I stood up and told everyone I was a Palmette."

"That was a mighty fine moment, if you ask me. Your Gram would've been so proud."

"So was I." It was real pride, not the shield she'd used to protect her from people and their opinions. "Sure, my voice shook a little, but I was proud of the man I love and how much he loves me. Proud that I come from a family who cherishes love!" She rapped the stirring spoon against the pot.

Dotty sniffed and wiped her nose. "Now that's a Palmette speaking. Don't let anybody get in your way, girl. You go after him."

"But I don't know where he is."

Brad had skipped town a day after the reverend. Carolina suspected he was building a case against the preacher, but May-Lee had been so vague on the phone.

"I can't believe he left." She didn't even like saying the words.

"It ain't permanent, child."

"Can I bet my heart on that?" She knew full well she already had.

"Look out, child, that lid's hot!" Dotty grabbed a pot holder and lifted the pan while Carolina poured blueberries into a line of jars. The older woman wiped her hands on her apron. "You know, a man's got his pride too. And defending his woman's part of it. I'd say that reverend better be on the lookout."

Three days later, Carolina had almost give up. Her furniture, just arrived from Boston, wasn't about to fit in with Gram's antiques. "I think most of Boston is going to end up in the attic." With Shepherd gone, at least it was *her* attic now, and all the house and grounds around it.

"Our attic," she corrected.

She'd even unlocked the cottage with the spare key Brad had given her and transferred some of his books to the shelves in the library. "Now all I need is the man to go with them."

But there'd been no word. He'd been gone five days.

"Can you believe it?" Carolina asked Gram's portrait as she collapsed on the parlor sofa. "This time I'm the one who stays while everyone else runs away!"

The knock at the door had her trembling on her feet, anticipation shooting through her like a current. Brad had a key, her eager heart warned her, and he'd let himself in.

Then she recalled the one he'd left in her mailbox the day he'd moved into town. The one she carried around in the patch pocket of her shapeless cotton dress. Her fingers curled around it. *Please be him.*

"About time you got here, Lavalier." The joke fell flat.

He stood on the edge of a circle of light. All she saw was a hopelessly rumpled suit and a smudge of day-old beard on his jaw. She would have thrown her arms around him if he hadn't stood with his back to her, hands sunk in his pockets.

"See you got a moving van," he said, glaring at the boxy yellow truck on the edge of the drive.

Carolina waved away a moth flitting around the light. She needed no reminders of hopeless causes. So he thought she was going. She might just let him believe it. "At least you came to the front door."

"You knew I wouldn't stay away."

"Did I?" she replied, sauntering back down the hall, calling over her shoulder when he didn't follow. "Come on in. If you dare be seen with such a notorious woman."

Brad scowled at the night. It hurt to scowl. He wanted to know when she was heading back to Boston, how she planned to leave him. But he wasn't about to ask.

She'd acted as if everything were fine that night on the porch. It had been an Oscar-winning performance. Either she hadn't meant it when she'd said she didn't care about public opinion anymore, or the last five days had been harder on her than she'd expected. The van confirmed his worst fears. He should have been there with her, weathering the storm.

Instead he'd gone after Shepherd, tracking him down along with his money, building a case that would stick.

The door was still wide open. Carolina waited under the arch to the parlor, arms crossed, toe lightly tapping. She was mussed and disheveled and smelled as if she'd take a shower sometime in the last hour. Her hair was pulled back in a loose, low pony tail, the humidity making it frizz.

"Where have you been?" she asked casually, never looking directly at him.

He laughed dryly. That hurt in a number of places too. "I was coordinating efforts with our private detective."

"Ah. Am I still paying him?"

"I am. I had to find out where Shepherd stashed my other clients' money. We did. We've attached secret church bank accounts all over the South."

"A financial consultant might have come in handy for that," she murmured, pursing her lips.

She wandered into the parlor, trailing a hand over an antique sofa he was surprised to find still here. If she was moving soon, she'd have to get more organized. "The detective mapped out Shepherd's trail from the panhandle until he came here. I took it from there."

"You found Shepherd too?"

"Yes."

She turned, about to remark that Shepherd had been easier to track down than he had. She'd been after May-Lee for days to tell her where— "Brad!" Her face froze in horror. "What happened to you?"

He grimaced at her reaction, wincing at the pain the grimace caused. He'd forgotten about his temple—a cut on top of a bruise on top of an egg-sized swelling. "I told you. I caught up with the reverend."

"Or a fast-moving train!"

"Mind if I sit down?"

"I was about to insist! Don't you move until I get some iodine."

He wasn't going anywhere. And he wasn't sitting down until she was safely out of the room. He inched his way onto the sofa. There was a hitch in his chest when he breathed, probably his ribs. It wasn't easy taking a punch when your arms were pinned behind you by some devil in a shiny suit.

But he was home at last. He'd spent hours in hotel rooms, compiling affidavits on Shepherd's misled victims. The stories he'd heard. Who said life in small towns was dull?

And there was only one woman he wanted to share his life with.

But she'd turned him down flat, with all the subtle tenderness of a scalpel cutting out his heart. Five days later, he was still bleeding. Iodine wouldn't help.

Her touch might.

She bustled back in with a tray, bare feet shuffling the summer mats. Her nightgown was peach-colored satin covered with a matching robe. He'd never seen it before. It dawned on him they'd only spent two nights together. Amazing how much lifetime a man could live in a handful of hours.

And how much tea a woman could shovel into him in the name of medicine. "Carolina, I hate to turn down your hospitality but—"

"Hush."

He stayed hushed while she went back to the kitchen in search of the first aid box. He closed his eyes a minute, trying to keep track of the throbbing points of light going off behind his eyelids. Then he inhaled a sultry whiff of something good, something that made him smile. "Carolina."

"I said hush now. Let me look at you."

"Only if I can return the favor."

Hands planted on her hips, Carolina glowered at him, taking stock of the dirt on his clothes, the bruise over his eye, the smudge she'd mistaken for five o'clock shadow. "If I don't miss my guess, that was one jim-dandy right to the jaw."

She plopped down beside him, wringing out a wet cloth. "You confronted him again, didn't you? Tried to shout down Shepherd and his microphone."

Brad tried sitting up straighter. It didn't take long to decide that staying where he was was better than groaning at her feet. "He was holding a revival outside De Ridder. I had the evidence this time. A briefcase full."

"And he had his whole congregation to defend him."

"And those bodyguards he calls assistants."

"How many of them did you have to fight off?"

"Just the two gorillas."

She clucked and shook her head, her hair whispering against her back, that floppy peach bow.

Brad caught himself reaching for it and stopped. "It got results last time, didn't it?"

She slapped the cloth on his forehead and ignored his grimace. "Only a stubborn, lovesick, honor-bound fool would call being chased out of his home amid scandal, results."

So she *was* leaving town, he thought.

She patted the crusted blood around his bump. "Are you going to tell me what happened next, or do I have to torture you with tea and excruciating kindness?"

She was torturing him as it was. Too agitated to be gentle, she smiled grimly every time he winced. That didn't stop her from smelling like soap and flowers. Nothing would stop him from loving her.

She flounced around, tossing bandages onto the tea tray, opening age-encrusted bottles of smelling salts and Mercurochrome, acting as if the way her breasts filled out the soft satin cups of her nightgown was completely beside the point now.

Her robe gaped open. All she cared about was giving orders. "Look down, please."

"I am, darlin', I am."

The iodine stung like a son of a bitch.

"The story, please?" she asked sweetly.

"He saw me in the back of the tent and asked a couple of his friends to escort me outside."

"And you went."

"I'd called the local police before the revival even began. I'm not stupid."

"Just intelligent enough to get the tar beat out of you."

"Do you want to hear it or not?"

"Go ahead." She muttered to herself while snipping off a section of gauze.

"It wasn't a beating, just few cheap shots. This adds assault charges to fraud—ow!"

"Good," she replied bluntly, pressing an adhesive bandage firmly to the discolored bump. "I'm so glad you won your case."

"I haven't won yet." He was still pleading it. He'd lost what Carolina valued most, the proud shreds of a reputation he'd reduced to nothing. There was no way to win that back. But he could give her love. Would she take the trade?

• She loved the house too, and she was leaving it because of him. A man with any real honor would offer to load the furniture himself, no matter how many bruised ribs he had. A man of honor wouldn't even think of asking her to marry him again.

Which just went to show, his honor had gone the way of her reputation.

Thirteen

"This cut is nasty," she murmured, her touch gentling. "Was he wearing a ring?"

"Which one?"

Carolina winced, imagining the scene. "And while you were outside, I'll bet Shepherd had the whole congregation shouting hallelujah's to cover the noise."

"Can't rightly remember."

"Uh-huh. Amnesia too. I thought so."

"I remember the important things."

Like the fact he'd said he loved her? She had witnesses.

She also had no talent whatsoever for nursing. Luckily for him, tender loving care didn't require a degree.

The man was hurting from more than a few well-thrown punches; it didn't take a doctor to see that. He'd been beating himself up since the night on the porch, blaming himself for the fact a person couldn't keep a secret in this town.

"I remember asking you to marry me."

The gravel in his voice made her turn, her heart hammering. "I believe I turned you down."

"I deserved it."

"You've got to understand one thing."

"I did. I do now."

She took a quick, jerky breath and promised herself she wouldn't cry for sheer joy. "You do?"

"I should have realized you couldn't live in this town anymore. Give me a few weeks to pack up the practice. We'll go together."

Carolina could curse a blue streak when she got a mind to, but Gram's "Tarnation!" was the first word that popped out of her mouth. "Brad Lavalier, you need more than a fist to knock some sense into that stubborn head of yours. Pack up and move where?"

Her outburst stunned him. He was glad those blunt-edged scissors were back in the first aid box. "We'll go to Boston," he suggested, with more conviction than he felt. The woman had more sides to her than a Rubik's Cube.

"No. We're not going to Boston."

"New York? New Orleans? Dammit, 'Lina, stop shaking your head." It was making him dizzy, and the room was none too steady to start with. "I want to marry you."

"Then you'd better get started listening to me. I love you. I'm proud of you." She stopped right there.

That was it? Brad had to walk, to pace, to get eye-to-eye with her so he wasn't looking up at a shimmering blur stalking across the carpet. He launched himself off the sofa and barely made it to the chair.

"You ought to be in bed."

"Not until I convince you to give me another chance."

"Bed's as good a place as any for convincing a woman."

"If a man said that, you'd slap him."

"Not if he was a man I loved."

He caught the last part, he just couldn't respond to it. The room was swimming, there were gray and green lights pulsing off to the side of his vision, and all that mattered was the purr of her voice. "Then why won't you marry me?"

"You haven't asked me. Not the right way."

"I'm in no shape for games, sugar."

"Then listen good. I love you and I always will. That's supposed to be a curse in our family, but Gram never thought so. Until I fell in love, really in love, I never knew why. I suspect that's because until I met you, I didn't know what love really was. This is that once-in-a-lifetime thing people dream about."

"And the whole town's talking about it. You didn't want that to happen."

"I didn't want to fall in love and be a typical Palmette either. I was wrong. Love is precious. When two people find it, it's no sin. It shouldn't be hidden. Shepherd's the one who should hide. Lying, stealing, cheating people."

"He'll never do those things again."

Her smile was glorious, wide as the dawn and sultry as the night. Brad's world righted a little—until she threw her arms around him and squeezed.

"I told you you were a hero," she said. "I'm so proud of you. Why, if my head gets any bigger, they're going to have to tie a string to it so it doesn't float away. As Dotty would say."

She kissed him smack on the lips. The groan he'd been holding on to finally escaped.

"Darlin', think I could breathe a bit?"

She stepped back, but not so far that her breasts weren't skimming his shirt, her hands petting his arms, his face, her eyes full of love. "The only thing you did wrong, Brad Lavalier, was make a proud woman prouder. And happier than any other woman in the world. Go ahead."

"And do what?" He loved her. With all his heart. And if he was still standing in five minutes, he'd tell her.

"Ask me to marry you again."

"Oh."

"Brad? Land sakes!"

He smiled, winced, and tried smiling with the other side of his mouth. One of these days, her accent was going to be as thick as Dotty's. "Sugar, will you ma—"

"Not now. Put your arm around me."

"I intended to."

"Not like that."

"Are you always going to be this bossy?"

"Only until I get you up to bed."

"Ah. The submissive type."

He was going to be out on his feet if she didn't get him upstairs soon. Gram had Doc Curtis's number tucked in that first aid box somewhere. Carolina would call him in a minute.

"I'm fine, really," he said when they at last reached the top of the stairs. "'Lina, if this bothers you, really, I can sleep in the cottage."

"When we just climbed all those stairs?" she asked with a laugh. She tucked an arm gingerly around his waist and walked him the last ten steps to the bedroom. "You sleep here. Besides, the cottage is closed up."

"You evicted me?"

"Nope. I moved you in here."

Sitting on the edge of the bed, it took him five minutes to figure out what should have been plain as day whenever she looked at him with love in her eyes—And pride straightening her backbone. "The van is for moving in, not out."

"You're quick, counselor."

"And you loved me all along."

"Just about." Before Brad, she'd tried so hard to hide her vulnerability with a show of strength, never guessing he hid a pugnacious streak behind his easygoing manner.

She pulled down the covers, slid off his jacket, and let him grouse about taking off his own pants. "I never thought you'd duke it out with the reverend."

"I'd do it all over again," he murmured. "If it ended

this way every time." He hitched an arm around her waist and brought her down on the bed with him. "You haven't kissed me yet."

"You haven't asked me."

"I'm asking."

Lips met lips, warmth and fears and growing joy mixed with sounds of the night.

"Brad, you're hurt."

"I'm healing fast."

"No more running," she said, "not for my sake. I love you and I want everyone to know it."

"As long as I know it, sugar. Tell me again."

Her lips did. She tasted sweet as peaches, tangy as a woman, as musky and uninhibited as a velvety Louisiana night.

"There's something else the whole town knows," she whispered.

"What?" He had trouble concentrating when she was unbuttoning his shirt.

"I'm planning a wedding."

"Anyone we know?"

She didn't dignify his question with a direct answer. Spreading his shirt wide, she gently kissed his chest, his abdomen, the indentation of his navel.

Although he couldn't breathe and reach at the same time, he managed to turn out the light before she saw the next set of bruises. He'd have them examined in the morning; right now there were more important things on his mind than scars of the past. There was a future to plan—and a night to spend in the arms of the woman he loved. "Are you taking that filmy thing off or am I?"

Carolina smiled in the dark. He thought she hadn't heard every labored breath as they'd climbed the stairs, every taut denial of pain. The man was sweet beyond words and brave beyond sense. And she loved him beyond all reason.

She'd humor him for an hour—one delicious, tender, unforgettable hour. Then she was calling the doctor.

"You just lie there and let me," she said, kneeling beside him on the bed, a flutter of satin landing somewhere in the dark. She skimmed his cheek with kisses, strummed his skin with her own.

Loving meant giving. That's what a trousseau was, what you brought to the one you loved when you were ready to make a home with him. Gram had known that. The people of Grelickville had too. Now Carolina knew it, all the way to her soul and back again. When the right man came along, you gave him everything you had.

Why? Because ever since Eve, the world had revolved around two people making love. That's what made life worth living. That's how life began.

THE EDITOR'S CORNER

For the best in summertime reading, look no further than the six superb LOVESWEPTs coming your way. As temperatures soar, what better way is there to escape from it all than by enjoying these upcoming love stories?

Barbara Boswell's newest LOVESWEPT is guaranteed to sweep you away into the marvelous world of high romance. A hell raiser from the wrong side of the tracks, Caleb Strong is back, and no red-blooded woman can blame Cheyenne Whitney Merit for giving in to his STRONG TEMPTATION, LOVESWEPT #486. The bad boy who left town years ago has grown into one virile hunk, and his hot, hungry kisses make "good girl" Cheyenne go wild with longing. But just as Caleb burns with desire for Cheyenne, so is he consumed by the need for revenge. And only her tender, healing love can drive away the darkness that threatens their fragile bond. A dramatic, thrilling story that's sensuously charged with unlimited passion.

The hero and heroine in SIZZLE by Marcia Evanick, LOVESWEPT #487, make the most unlikely couple you'll ever meet, but as Eben James and Summer Hudson find out, differences add spice to life . . . and love. Eben keeps his feet firmly planted in the ground, so when he discovers his golden-haired neighbor believes in a legendary sea monster, he's sure the gods are playing a joke on him. But there's nothing laughable about the excitement that crackles on the air whenever their gazes meet. Throwing caution to the wind, he woos Summer, and their courtship, at once uproarious and touching, will have you believing in the sheer magic of romance.

Welcome back Joan J. Domning, who presents the stormy tale of love lost, then regained, in RAINY DAY MAN, LOVESWEPT #488. Shane Halloran was trouble with a capital *T* when Merle Pierce fell hard for him in high school, but she never believed the sexy daredevil would abandon her. She devoted herself to her teenage advice column and tried to forget the man who ruined her for others. Now, more than twenty years later, fate intervenes, and Shane learns a truth Merle would have done anything to hide from him. Tempers flare but are doused in the sea of their long-suppressed passion for each other. Rest assured that all is forgiven between these two when the happy ending comes!

With her spellbinding sensuality, well-loved author Helen Mittermeyer captures A MOMENT IN TIME, LOVESWEPT #489. Hawk Dyhart acts like the consummate hero when he bravely rushes into the ocean to save a swimmer from a shark. Never mind that the shark turns out to be a diving flag and the swimmer an astonishingly beautiful woman who's furious at being rescued. Bahira Massoud is a magnificently exotic creature that Hawk must possess, but Bahira knows too well the danger of surrendering to a master of seduction. Still, she aches to taste the desire that Hawk arouses in her, and Hawk must walk a fine line to capture this sea goddess in his arms. Stunning and breathtaking, this is a romance you can't let yourself miss.

Let Victoria Leigh tantalize you with LITTLE SECRETS, LOVESWEPT #490. Ex-spy turned successful novelist I. J. Carlson drives Cassandra Lockland mad with his mocking glances and wicked come-ons. How could she be attracted to a man who provokes her each time they meet? Carlson sees the fire beneath her cool facade and stokes it with kisses that transform the love scenes in his books into sizzling reality. Once he breaches her defenses and uncovers her hidden fears, he sets out on a glorious campaign to win her trust. Will she be brave enough to face the risk of loving again? You'll be thoroughly mesmerized by this gem of a book.

Mary Kay McComas certainly lands her hero and heroine in a comedy of errors in ASKING FOR TROUBLE, LOVESWEPT #491. It all starts when Sydney Wiesman chooses Tom Ghorman from the contestants offered by the television show *Electra-Love*. He's smart, romantic, funny—the perfect man for the perfect date—but their evening together is filled with one disaster after another. Tom courageously sees them through each time trouble intervenes, but he knows this woman of his dreams can never accept the one thing in his life he can't change. Sydney must leave the safe and boring path to find the greatest adventure of all—a future with Tom. Don't miss this delectable treat.

FANFARE presents four truly spectacular books in women's popular fiction next month. Ask your bookseller for TEXAS! CHASE, the next sizzling novel in the TEXAS! trilogy by bestselling author Sandra Brown, THE MATCHMAKER by critically acclaimed Kay Hooper, RAINBOW by the very talented Patricia Potter, and FOLLOW THE SUN by ever-popular Deborah Smith.

Enjoy the summer with perfect reading from LOVESWEPT and FANFARE!

With every good wish,

Carolyn Nichols

Carolyn Nichols
Editor
LOVESWEPT
Bantam Books
666 Fifth Avenue
New York, NY 10103

NEW!

Handsome Book Covers Specially Designed To Fit Loveswept Books

Our new French Calf Vinyl book covers come in a set of three great colors— royal blue, scarlet red and kachina green.

Each 7" × 9½" book cover has two deep vertical pockets, a handy sewn-in bookmark, and is soil and scratch resistant.

To order your set, use the form below.